NIEKO'S TREASURE

JOY BUSSU

Published by Blushing Books
An Imprint of
ABCD Graphics and Design, Inc.
A Virginia Corporation
977 Seminole Trail #233
Charlottesville, VA 22901

Joy Bussu
Nieko's Treasure

eBook ISBN: 978-1-64563-816-2
Print ISBN: 978-1-64563-817-9
v1

R emisha Hughes sipped her drink quietly, watching her best friend and sister from another mister, Letecia read her latest work.

"You sure about this? I mean this is a big can of worms to open, Remy. You publish this story and he will come climbing out of the woodwork, he's going to think you're talking about him even if you're not," Letecia warned with a sigh, pushing Remisha's laptop back across the table to her.

"That's just it, Lettie. It's not about him. Everything I just described is everything I wanted and nothing he was, so there is no way he should think it's him," Remisha reasoned. "I need to do this, the magazine wanted a happy ending from me for once and I was actually able to write one. I honestly believe this story is me closing that chapter in my life," Remisha explained, picking up a chowder fry from the plate the waiter just set down in the center of their table.

Remisha and Letecia had been best friends since middle school. They were so inseparable they both left Alabama and went to college together at Xavier University in Louisiana and both relocated to Los Angeles after graduation.

Remisha graduated with a degree in creative writing and moved quickly up the ladder at the small publishing company she worked for and enjoyed her career as an editor. She also worked freelance as a writer.

Letecia moved to San Diego six years ago to further pursue her love of teaching and was currently the principal at a high school that was once known to have the lowest test scores and rating in the district. Since she'd taken over as principal the school's test scores were now in the top five and she was proud that all of the graduating class was accepted to either trade schools or colleges all around the world.

She was okay with the move because she was proud and happy for her best friend and, at the time, she had Clinton. They had been seeing each other for over a year and things were going well. Little did Remisha know her perfect relationship was about to implode and she would spend the next five and a half years being strung along by the biggest, selfish, douchebag God ever blew breath into.

Since the friends were so far apart now, they had a standing dinner date with each other two Fridays a month. They alternated who did the driving to the other, it was Letecia's turn to drive up and she begged to go to Cajun Cavern so here they were sitting out on the patio sipping amaretto sours and catching up on the last two weeks.

"I get it but I still think it's like poking a hornet's nest. Clinton Maxwell and his BS almost cost you everything the last time you dealt with him. You know the boy ain't wrapped too tight and he's gonna think it's him, are you sure you want to publish this story?" Letecia asked again, taking a fry of her own.

Remisha sighed and signaled their server for another drink for both of them. "Honestly, Lettie I'm tired of spinning in the mud I should have let dry years ago. I'm ready to let all that shit go once and for all, its time."

Clinton sipped his coffee and scrolled through the Essence website looking for Remisha's latest article/short story.

Of all his former loves, she was the only one he kept tabs on, because she was the one who got away. He still loved her as much as he always did and knew deep down inside she still loved him, too.

He always knew what she was up to because of her blogs and social media. After all he put her through he was surprised she never blocked him, but he also took it as a sign that there was hope for them.

Her social media was trending like crazy, her name and #Chocolate was popping up everywhere and had women from all over the world talking about needing some chocolate in their lives. When he heard the assistants talking about craving chocolate at lunch, followed by female laughter he knew he needed to see what the hype was all about.

His heart rate sped up when her picture came into view as he scrolled, she had changed her promo picture and her hair, he liked them both. The new picture looked like it was taken in a city park, blurred buildings were in the background, trees and grass in the forefront.

Her smile lit up her beautiful face, her hazelnut hued skin shined in the sun, her high cheekbones shimmered, he knew it was some sort of makeup but couldn't remember what it was called. Remisha didn't wear makeup when they were together so he wondered when she started wearing it and why, in his opinion she didn't need it; maybe he would mention that to her.

Her brown eyes were alight with laughter and bright, her naturally long eyelashes, he once accused her of being fake, framed them, her dark brown hair tumbled over her shoulders in curls. Her hair, like her lashes, was all hers and she alternated between curls like the ones in the picture or rocking her natural curls.

For once she decided to use a ¾ body picture so he was treated to a glimpse of her curves. Damn he missed her. Now that he thought about it, he didn't know how he felt about that though, he liked to think those were his curves and if he was checking them out so was every other man who had clicked on her article.

He had always thought she was one of the sexiest women he ever met and it looked like she was finally realizing it, too. She was a big, beautiful woman with a sexy ass body and in this picture she was showing it off and he didn't like it one bit!

Her beige slacks and peach, silk, button-down looked phenomenal on her and had him remembering how good she looked outside of her clothes too; that and the faint scent of peaches and mangos that followed her wherever she went.

He shook his head clear and scrolled past her picture and began to read her short story.

Immediately he knew exactly what she was talking about and soon a slow, cocky smile spread across his face, his baby had forgiven him! Yep it was past time for him to head out to Cali and check up on his number one girl.

"Girl, I can't believe how much attention that short story is getting, it's just a few paragraphs and now everyone keeps asking when the book is coming out, I'm like how about never people? I don't write books, I don't want to write books. Short stories are so much easier, in, out and done. Kind of like a one-night stand," Remisha told Letecia over the phone as she strolled through the mall after work.

She had a craving for an Auntie Anne's pretzel with spicy cheese dip and stopped to grab one. After she had her 'dinner' she decided to stroll through the mall and burn off some calories.

For a very long time Remisha hated everything about her body, she hated that while Letecia and the other girls in school could wear spandex and miniskirts she really couldn't without looking trashy. Things that rode their gentle hips and asses just right, clung to her like a second skin.

For years she starved herself on fad diets, tried everything from Weight Watchers to Paleo, worked out daily, sometimes twice a day trying to reach a magic number on the scale and when she got there she still hated how she looked and knew it was something bigger than her size.

Now, here she was five years later and she loved herself and every dimple and curve on her body and carried herself like a boss!

"Pshh, like you would know a damn thing about a one-night stand," Letecia scoffed in her ear. "And I hear you about not wanting to write a book, Remy, but you might want to reconsider, girl. You gave every woman in the world a sweet tooth, specifically for chocolate," Letecia said. Remisha could tell she was in her car by the echo on her end of the connection.

"Nah, I wrote the short, it's over and time to move on to the next one. Anyway, when I drive up next weekend, can we do a girls' night in? I'm talking movies, jammies and junk food. I need a wind down for real," Remisha suggested, stepping into an African gifts and crafts store, it was a great place to kill time and she wasn't ready to go home yet. She sighed contentedly as the scents of Nag Champa incense and scented oils surrounded her.

"Saturday we can, but we are meeting at that new Brazilian steakhouse on Friday, remember? Brent is coming too, he said he misses his sister-in-law and you keep sneaking in and out of town when he ain't here."

Remisha shook her head, smiling at the thought of Letecia's husband. If there was any man on this earth who was perfect for Letecia it was Brent. From day one she could see the chemistry between the two of them and was so happy for them both from the start.

"Tell my favorite pilot and brother-in-law it is not my fault he decided to start rubbing elbows with the big dogs and flying for Emirates Airlines and fine, Saturday for the night in, I'll need it after the steak house if it's anything like the one here," Remisha said reaching for a mini dress with embroidery that would match the new sandals she bought the other day, perfectly.

She walked over to the trifold of mirrors and held it up to herself, before turning around to go find a salesperson and bumped right into a tall frame with a wall of muscles so hard she stumbled back, landed on her butt and her air pod popped out.

"Damn, I'm so sorry. Are you all right?" a deep and sexy voice asked.

Remisha snatched her air pod off the floor and looked up with a glare, right before her heart jumped in her throat as Letecia continued to scream her name in her ear.

The equally tall and solid man looking down at her was fine as hell! He was at least 6'2" tall, his hair was cut into a bald fade, his deep, dark brown skin glowed in the store's artificial light.

His face was baby smooth except for a mustache. His eyes were piercing and dark, his lips were full and framed the most perfect set of teeth she had ever seen on a man in her life, and he was like a wall of a man! Barrel chest, muscular thighs and calves but not in a gym rat, bodybuilder way, he was just cut and massive in size.

He reached down to help her back to her feet.

"Lettie, let me call you right back. I just made a fool of

myself and bumped into someone," Remisha said, before quickly hanging up the phone, as she took his hand and he helped her to her feet.

"You never answered, are you okay?" he asked, smiling down at her watching her readjust her pencil skirt.

Remisha still felt her face burning from blushing, she looked up at him nodding. "Yeah I'm good, sorry I ran into you, I was busy running my mouth to my best friend, something I do often, especially when I'm out and about killing time," she over explained nervously, shaking the wrinkles out of the mini dress she wanted to try on, this man was the very definition of eye candy.

"I see," the stranger said, his gaze swept over her entire body before resting on the dress she was nervously swinging in her hand. "Are you going to try that on?" he asked her leaning against the wall next to the mirrors.

Remisha lightly touched the dress looking at him curiously. "That was the plan, do you work here or something?" she asked with a small smile.

He took the dress from her hands and turned to walk away, assuming she would follow him. "No, I own the place actually, just happened to be passing through after a meeting nearby and wanted to see how things were going," he explained, still walking away from her clutching the mini dress. He came up short when he realized she was still planted in front of the mirrors looking at him with a frown.

"Something wrong, Miss? Ah, forgive me, I never introduced myself." He came back over to her extending his hand. "Nieko. Nieko King and you are?" he asked, shaking her hand when he was stepping back in front of her, his friendly, sexy smile had her mouthwatering.

Remisha reached out taking his hand, surprised at his firm but gentle grip. "Remisha Hughes, nice to meet you. Now, please excuse me if this seems rude, but how can I be sure what you're telling me is the truth? This could be just a clever pick-up line," she answered, eyeing him skeptically but still digging his vibe.

Nieko continued to smile, his eyes taking another leisurely stroll up and down her curves. "If that were the case, Miss Hughes, I would have waited until you tried the dress on to make my move, because if you look even half as good in it, as I imagine you will, I have every plan of asking you out for dinner tonight," he quipped catching his bottom lip in between his teeth. His eyes on the move again.

"Remisha, and oh, really? So what if I look like a hot mess in the dress, Mr. King? What happens then?" she asked, folding her arms and trying not to squirm under his sexy ass gaze.

He rubbed his chin, the playful expression on his face turned to one of deep thought. "You can call me Nieko and if that were the case, which I highly doubt, we will comb this store together until you find something you like. But, in my opinion, there is nothing in this store that measures up with how beautiful and sexy you are, Remisha," Nieko informed her, turning again but waiting until she fell in step behind him this time to lead the way to the dressing rooms.

"Wow, thank you. Straight, no chaser, huh, Nieko?" Remisha blushed and followed him to the dressing room enjoying the view of his muscular back and ass. She was so distracted she failed to notice when he stopped walking and she over corrected at the last second, tripping over her feet.

Nieko turned around and made sure she was okay before handing her the dress. "I'm not one to beat around the bush or mince words, you know you're an attractive woman and I wanted you to know I noticed it too. There is nothing sexier in this world to me than a woman who loves herself, it just shines through and the light that you shine Remisha is breathtaking," Nieko told her, making her blush even more.

"You do realize you have only been talking to me for about ten minutes, right? You have given me enough ego stroking to last me a lifetime and you don't even know me. As much as I am enjoying it, don't you have work to do?" she asked, slipping into the dressing room.

"I am working, I'm helping you," Nieko answered through the closed door before wandering to a rack close to the dressing rooms and organizing the mask display on top of it.

"Yeah, I appreciate that but aren't we done now? I needed to find the dressing rooms, you brought me to them, so now you can continue 'checking on things' as you put it a few minutes ago, I'd hate to hold you up any longer," Remisha stated quickly shedding her clothes and trying on the dress, she loved how she looked in it and how it hugged her curves.

For a brief moment she actually debated on opening the door and letting him see her in it and getting his opinion, then she quickly changed her mind and started to get back into her clothes. She liked how she looked in it and it was her opinion that mattered most.

"No, we're not done, Remisha. I'm actually enjoying your company and would like to continue our conversation over dinner, get to know each other better?" Nieko asked moving to the next rack and display while he waited for her.

Remisha stepped out of the dressing room and wandered over to him smiling.

"Maybe one day, but tonight, I think I'll just take the dress. Nice to meet you, Nieko." She winked before walking over to the nearest attended cash register and made her purchase. She could feel his heated gaze still on her as she thanked the cashier and put her card back in her wallet and was not surprised when he stepped up to her as she walked to exit the store.

"Have a good evening, Remisha. It was a pleasure meeting you," he said, his sexy smile still in place as he handed her his business card. "Let me know when you can take me up on my dinner invitation." Nieko reached out to shake her hand again.

"You as well, Nieko. I will let you know. Goodnight," Remisha answered leaving the store and then the mall. Climbing into her car she looked down at his business card and dropped it in her middle console without much thought.

Nieko King was just her type but she had no desire in pursuing anything with him or anyone else, at the moment. No matter how much he looked like all of her fantasies of dark chocolate come to life.

Chapter 2

"Like I was telling Letecia, even with my new work schedule it seems like you kicked me to the curb. What's up with that, Sis?" Brent asked Remisha moving his plate and picking up his tongs so their server could carve him some lamb.

The new Brazilian restaurant did not disappoint, Remisha was so impressed by the fully stocked salad and antipasto bar that she almost forgot there was also meat.

"Oh please, don't even try it, Broski. I am out this way twice a month and you know it's been like this forever. So it's not my fault but whoever is making your schedule, the haters!" Remisha sniped, cutting into the sausage on her plate.

"Okay, okay, I'll give you that one, but seriously, Remy when are you just going to give up the ghost and move down here with us? I mean you don't have any family or anything holding you in Los Angeles." Brent pushed half of his lamb on Letecia's plate, something he always did when he thought something was really good. You need more protein now anyway," he told her when she gave him a dirty look.

Remisha noticed the pointed wide-eyed look Letecia shot

Brent's way and narrowed her eyes at them both. "All right, spill it. First Brent is trying to get me to move down here like I haven't been alone in Los Angeles since y'all moved here and now Lettie needs more protein, not more food but protein specifically, so what's up?" Remisha demanded, setting her fork and knife down eying them both suspiciously.

Letecia reached over taking Remisha's hand. "We just found out I'm pregnant," Letecia explained, a small, shy smile on her face while she waited for Remisha to react.

"Oh. My. God! It's about damn time! Had me waiting forever! I get to be a Godmommy and an Auntie!" Remisha said, dancing happily in her chair.

Letecia sighed looking relieved. "So you're really happy for us, Remy?" she asked nervously, squeezing Remisha's hand.

Remisha looked at her like she was crazy. "What the hell kind of question is that, Lettie? Of course I'm happy for you guys! You are my best friend and my sister from another mister so come again, say what?"

Letecia's bottom lip started trembling as tears fell from her eyes. "I don't know what's wrong with me, I was just so worried you would be upset after– well, you know, or feel left out," Letecia explained using her napkin to wipe away her tears.

"Lettie, why would you even allow thoughts like that to take root? I have been there and genuinely happy for everything good that happens in your life and fighting mad for everything bad. That will never change and you know it. You two are my family and now I get a baby to spoil too? Yasss! I am all in!"

Brent covered both of their hands and started rubbing Letecia's back as tears still slowly rolled down her face. "She found out today that she has anemia and might be having multiples, so she can't travel up to Los Angeles anymore," Brent explained, smiling at Letecia.

"Okay and? I have no problem driving here to see you guys and when she gets closer to giving birth I can move down for a few months or whatever you guys need me to do. So can we stop all of this emotional mess so I can order a glass of champagne to celebrate *my* baby or babies, please?" Remisha asked, signaling their server to order her drink before hugging Letecia tight.

"You know you're going to be putting miles on miles, right? I want you here for everything, from the ultrasound to the birth! I need you, Remy."

Remisha thanked their server for her glass of champagne and looked at Brent with an arched eyebrow when he asked him to leave the bottle and requested two more glasses.

"You ain't said nothing but a word Lettie and don't trip. I'm here for all of it. I can't wait to start shopping for my baby or babies! When will we really know if there is more than one? And when will we know if you're having a girl or a boy?" Remisha asked, taking a sip and looking at Brent like he was crazy when he set a quarter full glass of champagne in front of Letecia before pouring his own. "Have you lost your mind? She can't drink anymore!" She scolded and reached out to take it away but Letecia was quicker.

"Remy calm the hell down I can have an occasional glass of wine. I can already tell you are going to be worse than Brent!" Letecia snapped, shaking her head.

"But that's not wine, it's champagne," Remisha argued, shaking her head.

Letecia took a small sip to spite Remisha. "Oh good Lord, calm down," she quipped laughing at Remisha's hostile glare before looking over at the entrance of the steakhouse, her smile dropping to a disgusted look. "Can someone please tell me why Clinton Maxwell's shady ass is walking this way?"

Remisha looked over her shoulder in alarm and sure enough, the man who was once every dream come true but turned out to be her worst nightmare was headed their way.

Remisha finished her glass of champagne and quickly poured another one.

"Well, well, well, who would have thought when I came out to grab a bite to eat on my vacation, I'd run into my number one girl and two of her favorite people?" Clinton said, smiling at the three of them.

In true best friend fashion, Letecia glared at him looking ready to take his head off, Brent went into big brother mode and looked menacing and Remisha just poured another glass of champagne looking over her shoulder at him.

"I know this cheating ass scrap of a man didn't just call you his number one girl, acting like shit didn't happen, did he? Letecia asked, glaring and rolling her eyes in Clinton's direction. After all he put Remisha through, there most definitely was no love lost between Clinton and Leticia, she pretty much hated his ass.

"Yep, girl that is exactly what he tried to say, but considering the fact I am not his anything anymore, there must be another poor unfortunate soul in this place tonight who fell for the Clinton Maxwell bullshit program," Remisha snapped looking Clinton up and down like he smelled bad.

"Damn, it's like that, Remisha? I thought we were past all of that, the last time we talked you told me you finally forgave me," Clinton said, still smiling like he won the lottery.

"True, I said I forgave you. I did that for me but I didn't say a word about liking you. Now if you will excuse us we are trying to enjoy our dinner, and you are killing our vibe," Remisha told him with a plastic smile.

"Still all about the jokes, huh, Remy? I'll let you have that one because we both know where your heart is. I'll be in touch," Clinton told her before moving towards the bar to pick up his order.

"See Remy? I told your ass you keep poking around in tall grass and eventually a snake will come slithering out and you done messed around and attracted their fucking king!" Letecia snapped, referring to Remy's most recent short story, then going back to sipping her champagne.

"Remisha, you have a delivery at the front desk," the receptionist told her on the intercom the following Tuesday. She was curled up in the giant, foam, bean bag chair in the corner of her office reading over a new author's manuscript. That was one of the great things about her job, she pretty much made her own hours and got to come and go as she pleased. As long as she got her work done, they left her to her own devices.

Remisha set her laptop and notebook aside and slipped on her sandals before walking to the front desk with a bit of a frown, she rarely received packages especially at work.

She came up short when she saw a huge, stuffed snow leopard holding flowers sitting in the lobby chair closest to the receptionist desk. She walked around and plucked the card pinned to the stuffed animal's ear and immediately felt annoyed, Clinton Maxwell and his game playing ass. She snatched the animal up so fast the flowers fell to the ground and the receptionist Elisha gasped in surprise.

"Oh no, they were such beautiful flowers too!" she said, standing up and looking over the desk at the scattered petals on the carpet. "I hope some of them are salvageable." Elisha sighed and sat back down to answer the ringing phone.

Remisha smiled at Elisha, gathering the remnants of the flowers and tossing them in the nearest trash can before carrying the snow leopard to her office and depositing it in her office chair on her way back to her laptop and bean bag. She balled up the card in her fist and tossed it in the trashcan next to her.

His simple message 'Miss you much' would have touched

her if she didn't know Clinton as well as she did and all she had been through because of him.

"Okay, I know I said I am willing to go above and beyond for you and my baby and or babies but, girl, this can't be an ongoing thing. I have been in this car so long my butt is numb," Remisha complained a month later, finally climbing out of the driver's seat of her car. Moving her feet up and down to get the circulation going in her legs again.

Letecia called her close to tears because she was craving crab cakes from their favorite spot but she wanted them fresh, otherwise they would be cold and soggy by the time Remisha got them to her. So as only a true best friend would, she drove to San Diego to pick up Letecia to take her to grab her crab cakes.

"I know and I'll try my best to keep it to a minimum. But I tried, Remy, I really did. I ordered crab cakes from six different places in the last few weeks and none of them tasted right," Letecia explained, putting her sunglasses on top of her head, and linking arms with Remisha as they walked into Cajun Cavern.

"Maybe they taste funny now because of the pregnancy," Remisha reasoned with maddening logic.

"Girl, no! The horror! Can you imagine?" Letecia exclaimed, pressing her hand to her chest as Remisha told the new hostess they were a party of two and they wanted to sit outside. They knew she was new because they ate there so much all of the staff knew both of them by their first names.

"It happens though, so if these crab cakes aren't the manna from Heaven you remember, then more than likely it's the pregnancy hormones messing with your tastebuds." Remisha fell in step behind the hostess leading them to their table.

They were led to their favorite table in the corner and needlessly passed menus, they always ordered basically the same things each time they came. The only difference was amaretto sours were no longer an option.

The warm sea breeze moved around them, causing Remisha to sigh contentedly staring out at the water for a moment before she picked up her water glass to take a sip, looking around the patio and her eyes met with those of the very handsome Nieko King.

A sexy smile moved across his handsome face as he nodded in acknowledgement in her direction. The giddy feeling she had the first time she saw him returned, moving into her stomach like butterflies.

Letecia followed her line of vision, looking over her shoulder before looking back at Remisha with a questioning look. "Damn! He's fine! Who is that, Remisha?" she asked, looking over her shoulder again to get a better look at Nieko.

Remisha took a deep breath, shaking her head, her gaze dropped to the menu in front of her on the table. "Nieko King. I met him a while back at the African Gifts store in the mall," she explained, she purposely left out the part about him asking her out and her leaving him hanging.

"Are you sure all you did is meet? That man is looking at you like you are his last meal, girl. You better feed that man!" Letecia teased, drinking her water.

"Lettie, what the hell? I don't know a damn thing about that man, let alone anything that would make me want to 'feed' him as you so eloquently put it," Remisha admonished, trying to decide between her two favorites, the Cajun pasta and jambalaya.

"Whatever, Remy, you just need to stop being so damn evil! So, I'm thinking I'm getting two orders of crab cakes, is that too much?" Letecia asked looking over at Remisha with a small smile.

"Word to the wise, order one, see if you even want those before we end up wasting food, and for the record, I am not evil. I just know what I want." Remisha's breath caught in her chest when she saw Nieko stand from his table and move their way.

"Remisha Hughes," was all he said when he approached their table looking down at her smiling. "The woman who has yet to take me up on my dinner invitation, good to see you again and still looking as beautiful as the first day I saw you." His face took on a hint of annoyance when he mentioned the fact he hadn't heard from her.

Remisha looked at him failing miserably at fighting the blush that moved across her face. Her eyes took a leisurely stroll up his tall frame to his handsome face. No, the snapshots she'd saved in her mental rolodex of him were not embellished, Nieko King was freaking gorgeous!

She had moved his business card from the middle console of her car to her wallet but still hadn't mustered up the nerve to call him. After Clinton, Remisha learned men who looked like Nieko were great to look at but not to try to build relationships with.

"Nieko King, the stroker of egos and seller of beautiful dresses," Remisha quipped, ignoring his statement about her not calling. She directed his attention to Letecia and tried to get her thoughts together under his intense gaze. "Let me introduce you to my best friend, Letecia."

Nieko extended his hand to Letecia with a warm smile. "Nice to meet you, Letecia. I guess it is true what they say about birds of a feather and all, you are just as beautiful as your friend here."

Letecia took his hand and shook it, looking from him to Remisha and back again blushing slightly. Happily married or not it always felt good to know that not only Brent thought she was beautiful.

"Nice to meet you too and the stroker of egos is most definitely a spot-on description for you. So tell me, how did you meet my lovely friend here and what are your intentions with her?" Letecia asked with an arched eyebrow and a smirk.

"Lettie! Nieko please excuse her, she is pregnant, and hungry but most importantly she has no filter, never has," Remisha quickly explained, shooting daggers at Letecia.

Nieko chuckled looking down at the two of them. "No worries, Remisha, I actually appreciate her directness. To answer your questions, Letecia, we met at my African gift store in the mall and as far as my intentions with Remisha... Would you ladies mind if I joined you for lunch? I would be more than willing to discuss my intentions further, especially since it looks like your server is here to take your orders anyway." Nieko moved to the side standing closer to Remisha's side of the table, his eyes on her once again.

"I think that is a great idea, Nieko. Please have a seat and I would like two orders of crab cakes and the mixed greens side salad, please," Letecia smiled at the waiter handing him back her menu before smiling at Nieko.

"Is it okay with you too, Remisha?" Nieko asked politely, looking down at her again.

Remisha shot one last withering look in Letecia's direction before smiling at Nieko. "Sure, I don't mind, Nieko." She gestured to the empty chair to her right. "Have a seat and I'll have the Cajun pasta." Remisha handed the waiter back the menu.

Nieko settled in the chair, winking at her. "Make that two Cajun pastas and a bucket of crawfish too, please."

The waiter added his order to his notepad and rushed over to the table Nieko had vacated bringing his drink, and silverware and setting it up in front of him. "I'll get your orders put in, are you ladies having amaretto sours this afternoon?" the waiter asked them knowingly.

"If I may?" Nieko sat up looking at each of them in turn, holding up a finger to let them all know he was going to order for the table. "Two virgin white linens and one Jameson and the Giant please." The waiter made a note and walked away from their table with a nod.

"And what if I wanted an amaretto sour?" Remisha asked Nieko, looking annoyed after the waiter walked away.

"Because I saw the look on your face, you were about to decline and stick to water," Nieko answered sitting back again, not fazed by her annoyed look. "So I suggested an alternative."

"Nieko, you don't know anything about me besides my dress size, so don't sit here acting like you do," Remisha snapped, drinking all of her water and rolling her eyes at Letecia, this was all her damn fault for inviting this damn man to their table by asking about his intentions!

A devious smile lit up his face as he picked up his own water glass. "True, but isn't that one of the benefits of me joining you two for lunch? Getting to know each other better?" he countered looking at Letecia before returning his hot gaze to Remisha.

"Actually you joined us so you could tell Letecia's nosy ass more about your intentions, I would have been perfectly fine with you returning to your own table," Remisha answered, still looking more than a little rebellious.

"Ahh, so you're not curious at all, Remisha?" he asked, the same smile plastered on his face.

"Nope. Just along for the ride and the food," she lied with a serious face, yes she was curious! She wanted to know more about him, especially since he took over and ordered their drinks, having him take control over something so simple had piqued her interest in a different way.

"Remy, stop being so damn evil! Nieko, I can assure you as her best friend for life or longer, if she wasn't interested in what you had to say, you wouldn't be sitting here," Letecia told

Nieko shaking her head at Remisha. "So back to my original question, what are your intentions with my evil friend?" Letecia laughed at the visual death threat Remisha was sending her way before directing all of her attention to Nieko.

"Honestly, Letecia I think Remisha is a very beautiful woman and at this moment in time, I want to get to know her better, much better if she'll allow it. I had hoped my chance to do so would have occurred by now but Remisha has chosen a slower route and, for the record, I don't view her reluctance towards me as malicious or even spiteful, she is all about guarding her heart and I respect that," Nieko informed Letecia before casting another glance at Remisha. "But of course you being her best friend and knowing her better than I do, I could be wrong."

Letecia nodded thoughtfully. "Interesting. You do realize if this acquaintanceship was to continue I will hold you to the very highest of standards, I don't take Remisha's happiness lightly, and winning her heart won't be easy," she warned.

Nieko nodded, smiling even brighter at Letecia, it seemed he reserved his devious, yet sexy, smile for Remisha. "As you should and from what I've seen so far, I welcome the challenge."

Remisha's glare bounced between the two of them as their waiter brought their drinks to the table. "You two do realize I have some say in this as well, right?" she snapped, cautiously picking up the glass in front of her.

"Would you be you if you didn't, Remisha?" Nieko asked, taking a sip of his drink, his eyes moving all over her face and body.

Remisha narrowed her eyes in his direction. "Okay that is now three times you have spoken in absolutes about me and again I have to say, you don't know a thing about me, Nieko," Remisha countered taking a small drink from her glass, she hated to admit it but the drink was delicious.

"Well why don't we change that? Better yet, in the spirit of getting to know each other better, let me tell you something about myself, I like to play games. As a matter of fact are you up to play one with me now?" Nieko challenged, his devious smile returning as his gaze raked over her again.

"Playing games, huh? I have to say, Nieko, that's not something most men would admit to coming right out the gate, or even at all," Remisha told him, taking another drink. Letecia sat back watching the back and forth between them.

"Are you going to play Remisha?" he asked, ignoring her snide comment altogether.

Remisha looked over in question at Letecia, who shrugged her shoulders bringing her drink to her lips. Remisha could tell Letecia was enjoying seeing her in the hot seat. Normally her sharp tongue and words had men running for the hills within minutes of meeting her, Nieko seemed to almost welcome them both.

"What kind of game are you trying to play, here?" Remisha asked, sitting back in her chair looking over at him with a frown, but very intrigued.

"A simple one, let's call it an icebreaker, you down?" Nieko still had the same devious smile on his face, like he had her painted in a corner and was enjoying it.

"You know what, why not? Let's play. I'm actually kind of curious to see what you're up to," Remisha answered, squirming a little, damn, those looks he kept casting her way were getting to her.

Nieko's smile got even more devious. "Okay, so here's the deal, I'm going to tell you what I've learned about you just from the two times we've met. If I'm right, I'm taking you to dinner tomorrow, if I get even one thing wrong, we will continue this thing at the snail's pace you seem to be a fan of, deal?" Nieko propositioned taking another sip of his drink, waiting for her to answer.

Letecia picked up her own glass and took a drink waiting on Remisha's next move. "This is pretty good, Nieko what's in it?" Letecia asked, bringing the glass closer to her face.

"Cucumber, mint, simple syrup, lime, and soda water in this case. Ketel one and St Germain is added when it's alcoholic. I figured if you enjoyed amaretto sours, you would enjoy white linens as well," Nieko told Letecia before redirecting his attention back to Remisha. "Well, Remisha, do we have a deal?"

Remisha sipped her drink slowly thinking about his 'game', on one hand she knew it was impossible for him to know much of anything about her but on the other hand she was in a catch-22 when it came to the end results. As much as she kept telling herself she didn't want to start something with Nieko, her senses were saying something completely different. In the short time he had been sitting with them, he'd intrigued her enough to want to know more, need to know more.

"We have a deal as long as you promise not to renege when you lose," Remisha challenged, giving Nieko a deadpan look. "Tell me all you know about me from knowing me for all of ten whole minutes, Nieko. I am dying to hear this."

Nieko's face lit up with the same devious smile. "Let's see, starting with the first time we met, you are very confident and don't care about anyone else's opinion, especially concerning your clothes. That being said, it wasn't always that way though, you used to dress to please other people not yourself," Nieko said, pausing as their waiter came back to the table with condiments for Letecia's crab cakes, an empty bucket and wet naps for Nieko, and extra napkins.

Remisha arched an eyebrow looking over at Letecia who was sporting a huge grin. In the short time he'd been at their table, Remisha could tell he already had Letecia's vote. So far so good, he was absolutely correct. She was still debating on making sure he lost, regardless of what he said, just to take some of the wind out of his sails. He was already too damn cocky for his own damn good.

"Anything else?" she asked, ignoring Letecia's smirk in her direction.

"Remisha, rest assured I just got started. Let's move on to today. You noticed me almost from the moment you sat down and pretended you didn't even after Letecia caught you staring at me, why? Because then you would have to admit that even though you are interested in me and I asked you out ages ago, you never took me up on the offer because of someone in your past and she would nail you to the wall about it." He paused again when the waiter came back with another server and set their plates in front of them. "And the drinks, from the minute you sat down I noticed how friendly the waitstaff is to you and Letecia, almost like old friends so they obviously know you well because you come here often. However, they haven't been made aware of Letecia's delicate condition or the waiter wouldn't have suggested the drinks. Now back to you, you are as protective over Letecia as she is over you, so two things. One, there is no way in hell you would even allow her to drink alcohol while she's pregnant and two, since this is both of your favorite place to wind down and chill, you wouldn't feel comfortable having a drink without her being able to have one, too. I'm even willing to bet money that the only time you come here is with Letecia as well," Nieko concluded, picking up the rolled napkin that contained his silverware.

He unrolled the cloth napkin and placed the silverware on the table, and the napkin in his lap, his eyes still on her. A glint of triumph flickered there.

Remisha grabbed her own silverware and took out a fork and knife to cut the shrimp in her pasta into smaller pieces, tripping that he had been right about *everything* he said about her. She took a small bite of her food before looking at him again, and almost choked on it when he sucked the juice from the head of the crawfish he just broke apart, his eyes meeting hers as he did it.

"So how'd I do?" he asked her knowing he was right, popping the tail of the crawfish in his mouth after peeling the shell off.

Remisha sighed in defeat. "What time should I be ready tomorrow?"

"So you're wearing that print dress right? The short one you bought from his store right?" Letecia asked Remisha the following day as soon as she answered the phone.

"Ugh! Don't you have a baby book to read or something? Dang! This would be a moot point if you hadn't gone all motherly and overprotective at Cajun's yesterday and Nieko would still be on simmer where I left his ass!" Remisha snapped, looking at the exact dress Letecia was suggesting laying out on her bed for her date.

"Remy, you hadn't even turned on the damn stove so you should be thanking me! You can act all mad if you want to, but you and I both know you're feeling that man so save that fake outrage for someone who doesn't know you so well. Shit, I guess that leaves Nieko out too!" Letecia teased, laughing hard.

"You are way past the proper mourning period for a relationship. Besides it's just dinner, if you don't want to see him again, don't see him again," Letecia snapped back. "Now back to your date outfit, you know those red platform heels of mine you still have will look amazing with that dress right? Just saying."

"Yeah, yeah, Lettie, you are always just saying, can I get back to work now?" Remisha fussed, she decided to work from home so she could work longer before getting ready for her date and not worry about her commute messing up her timeline.

"You do that but seriously, Remy, he's a nice guy, give the poor man a chance, damn!"

"Remisha, I need your address so I know when I have to leave my office to get us to dinner on time," Nieko explained patiently over the phone after she reminded him, via text, that he didn't need her address because she was driving herself.

Remisha shook her head, running her hand down her face before answering him, between Letecia and now him, she had yet to get any work done. "Nieko, like I told you yesterday, I'll just meet you there. You don't have to go through all of that trouble, it's not that serious," she told him, closing her laptop and moving it off of her lap.

"And like I told you yesterday, it is that serious, Remisha. I am not comfortable with that plan. The purpose of this date is for us to get to know each other a little better so I want you to be able to relax. What if you decide to have a drink or two this evening, how will you get home? I don't know what kind of men you are used to dating but I refuse to allow you to put yourself at unnecessary risk," he argued with an impatient sigh. "Now, since you have reservations about me coming to pick you up for whatever reason, I am willing to make one concession and only one, if I am not picking you up, a car service is," Nieko stated sternly.

Remisha was beginning to recognize Nieko didn't like to be challenged in things and liked to take charge, but after playing puppet for Clinton all those years she refused to give the strings to another man. She was tempted to tell him the date was cancelled, this was becoming too much of a damn headache!

"Nieko, I appreciate you wanting to look out for my safety but I–" she began to argue but he quickly cut her off.

"Remisha, as I said the car service is my only concession. If you are still trying to argue driving yourself, consider the issue closed. I'll have the service call you to arrange pickup or you can give me your address so I can pick you up, which is it going to be?" he demanded in a no-nonsense type of way.

Remisha leaned back against the wall behind her, closing her eyes, praying for patience. Just like in her office, her chair of choice to work in was her giant beanbag chair. "Nieko, maybe this isn't such a good idea, it's obvious you are used to a certain type of woman and I am not the shrinking violet type. So, yeah, I don't see this working out in the slightest," Remisha stated in a regretful tone. She was attracted to him, very attracted to him but she wasn't sure if she could ever get used to his demanding demeanor.

"I don't remember asking you to be anyone but yourself, Remisha. I asked you if I am picking you up or should I give the car service your information. It amazes me that my looking out for your safety on our date has been such a topic of debate. I'm simply doing what a man does or is supposed to do, anyway."

Remisha scoffed and pulled her phone from her ear, frowning at it before letting what he said sink in. What *was* so wrong with him wanting to make arrangements to ensure her safety for the evening? Now that she really thought about it, honestly nothing. She was just so used to looking after herself even when she was in relationships that when Nieko approached her with her needs in mind, it was uncomfortable and came off demanding instead of being considerate. Damn.

"You're absolutely right, Nieko, and if the offer still stands, please give the car service my information and I'll see you tonight?" she asked, hoping her stubbornness hadn't driven him away.

"Of course my offer still stands, Remisha. It would take more than that to make me reconsider getting to know you better. I'll have the service call as soon as we hang up and I look forward to seeing you tonight."

The car he sent for her pulled up in front of The Firehouse Restaurant at 6:30 on the dot that evening. The car service had been quick to inform her that they had strict instructions to have her at the restaurant by 6:30, so her pick-up time was scheduled accordingly.

Nieko stood outside waiting for her looking casually fine, he was wearing black jeans, a dark green Henley shirt and a black blazer. She couldn't help but smile at the fact he was her date for the evening, as he stepped forward and helped her out of the car.

"I hoped that was what you'd choose to wear tonight, you look amazing, Remisha," Nieko whispered in her ear, referring to the dress she bought from his store the day they met. He kissed her on the cheek and handed her a tiger lily in the same shade of orange as her dress before grabbing her other hand and leading her into the restaurant.

"Thank you, this is a really nice place, Nieko. Have you ever been here before?" Remisha asked smelling the flower, taking notice of a few women doing double takes as he led her to the bar area.

"No, this is my first time. I've always wanted to check it out but decided I'd wait for an occasion special enough, so here we are. Our reservation isn't until 7:30 but I figured we could sit at the bar and just talk for a bit, they know to come find us when our table is ready." He stepped up to a vacant table and pulled out her chair for her, before settling directly across from her.

Remisha laid her clutch and flower on the table beside her

smiling at him, she had no idea what kind of cologne he was wearing but it was holding an entire conversation of its own with her senses and hormones.

"Fine with me and I'm flattered you feel a first date with me is a special enough occasion to come here." She smiled over at him, again taking in how good he looked. After their heated conversation earlier, something in her shifted and now she genuinely wanted to know all she could about Nieko.

"I'm amazed you haven't figured out by now that any time I get to spend with you, Remisha is that special," Nieko replied, his dark eyes serious and intense. "Would you like a drink?" he asked, moving to stand and go to the bar.

"Sure, why not? It's Friday and I have a driver." Remisha smirked.

"That you do. I'll be right back," he said, moving to her side of the table and kissing her on the cheek again before going over to the bar. She was about to call out what she wanted to drink since he didn't ask her but remembering how he took control the day before she just sat back and let him choose for her.

Remisha watched him as he walked away, once again several women in the bar area took notice of him and a few repositioned themselves in an attempt to get his attention. Nieko's focused stride to the bar never faltered.

When he reached the bar and was talking to the bartender to place their order, a woman sitting on the stool next to where he was standing, reached out lightly touching his arm to get his attention. Remisha recognized her immediately, her name was Melissa and it took all the strength in her body not to cross the room, snatch the bitch off the stool and beat the shit out of her.

Nieko looked over the heavily made-up woman on the bar stool next to him touching his arm. Everything about her screamed easy and available. He would never understand why a woman felt the need to put herself out there that way. Men liked and were intrigued by the thrill of the chase, by a woman who guarded her secrets like the treasures they are.

"Can I help you, Miss?" Nieko asked her politely, getting the bartender's attention and moving away from her touch. "Let me get a gin and tonic and an amaretto sour please," Nieko ordered, still trying to get his wayward thoughts under control. The minute Remisha stepped out of that car all he wanted to do was grab her and push his tongue down her throat, she looked that damn good!

He was still tripping on how attracted he was to her. From the moment he saw her reflection in the mirror he knew he wanted her, now he was dying to know if she was looking for a relationship and if she would be open to the kind of relationship he had in mind.

"I was just going to offer to buy you a drink." The woman smiled at him seductively, letting her tongue peek out from between her lips, crossing her legs and leaning forward giving him a peek of her cleavage.

"Bring them to the table over there and I need to start a tab," Nieko instructed the bartender before moving away from the bar and the flirty woman.

"I'm good, enjoy your evening," he threw out with an uninterested tone in her direction as he made his way back over to Remisha. He could feel the woman's heated gaze on his back, not that he cared in the least. The woman he'd set his sights on was right in front of him looking like his every fantasy came true.

Remisha watched in disgust as Melissa licked her lips watching Nieko walk away and looked like she was about to follow him until she noticed he sat across from her. She immediately glared at Remisha and turned back around facing the bar again, tossing her hair over her shoulder angrily.

Nieko noticed the exchange but didn't say anything about it as he sat back down. "Remisha, tell me about yourself," he requested, taking her hand in his across the table.

"Hell, after your little game last night, why don't you tell me all about myself?" Remisha teased, thanking the server who just arrived at their table and set an amaretto sour in front of her and a tumbler of white liquor and ice in front of Nieko.

"I believe I exhausted my knowledge of all things Remisha yesterday to get this date, so you will have to indulge me and tell me more." Nieko leaned forward and placed a gentle kiss on the back of her hand. The contact of his lips on her, sent her hormones into orbit!

Remisha crossed her legs to combat the rhythmic thumping rising between them and took a gulp of her drink looking over at him, letting the flavor dance on her tongue before she swallowed it.

"How do they measure up to the amaretto sours at Cajun's?" Nieko asked, running his thumb across the top of her hand.

Remisha took another sip, savoring the taste more this time. "It's pretty good actually." Remisha nodded looking impressed at the drink in her hand.

"Good to hear it, now back to you." He took her other hand, kissing that one too.

Remisha bit the inside of her cheek to keep from moaning, his soft ass lips were about to be the death of her and all he'd done was kiss the back of her hands!

"Let's see, I'm originally from Alabama, thirty-two, I have a degree in creative writing and have been with Light and Love

Publishing Company for the last eight years," she told him. Taking one of her hands away from his to take another sip of her drink, she felt someone looking at her and turned her head to look for the source and was met with Melissa's more than hostile glare. If Remisha had to guess, Melissa just figured out who she was.

"Friend of yours?" Nieko asked, following her gaze, smiling like he just won the lottery.

"Not hardly and I could ask you the same thing, she's been shooting daggers my way since you left her at the bar." Remisha used the small straw to stir the ice around in her glass to melt it a little bit.

Nieko looked from Remisha to Melissa several times almost in a comic-like fashion. "I have no idea who that woman is and I assure you, the only woman I am interested in is you, here or otherwise. Now, please continue, I'm intrigued," he assured her, bringing her hand to his lips again.

The rhythmic pulse between her legs picked up to an incessant pace causing her to shift in her seat. Remisha pulled her hands away shaking her head.

"Okay, I'm going to need you to stop doing that and what more do you want to know about me?" she asked, instantly regretting leaving the topic so far open when she saw his devious smile from the day before return.

"Everything," he answered, drinking from his glass looking at her intently to continue, his sexy dark eyes narrowed a little.

"I see, well that could take a while. I have an idea, yesterday you said you like to play games, right? So what about this? You get to ask me three questions and I get to ask you three questions, that way we get to know each other at the same time and neither one of us is monopolizing the conversation," Remisha suggested, looking over her shoulder at the glaring woman again. She did a double take when she saw who was now standing next to Melissa getting all of her attention, none other than Clinton Maxwell.

She wasn't a jealous person especially not about Clinton but seeing them together after everything she'd been through because of them had her seeing red. At least now she knew it was Melissa that brought him back to California and not her short story, so no more 'I told you so's' from Letecia!

Remisha felt her face grow hot from memories of the past surging forward. Together they put her through so much emotional turmoil she never thought she'd heal from it all, and it cost her $8,000 to fix the paint job on her car from Melissa's damage, and for what? Because Clinton was cheating on them both? All these years later, she still didn't understand how any of that was her damn fault.

Nieko followed her line of vision, reached over and grabbed her hand again to recapture her attention. "Old friends or unfinished business?" he asked with a nod of his head in Clinton and Melissa's direction.

Remisha's gaze shifted back to Nieko and she dropped her head, shaking off the bad vibes seeing the two of them caused her. "Neither. Ex-boyfriend and the woman I caught him cheating with, and I just had a flashback of my BMW," she explained looking at Nieko, her smile returning instantly.

Nieko frowned, looking a bit confused, he opened his mouth to speak when a server walked over to tell them their table was ready. He stood and walked over to Remisha and extended his hand to help her out of her seat.

He kept her hand in his grasp as she gathered her clutch and flower to follow the server. Nieko turned back to the couple at the bar with a curious glance, noticing that the man's eyes were narrowed as he watched them leave the bar area. Nieko gave them both a head nod before resting his hand on the small of Remisha's back, letting her fall in step beside him.

He saw the look of regret in the man's eyes and the flash of jealousy in the woman's. "Sucks to suck," Nieko muttered under his breath, shaking his head at the stupidity of some men.

"What did you say?" Remisha asked, her beautiful face lit up in a content smile as he pulled her chair out for her once they reached their table.

"Nothing important, beautiful, just tripping on human nature and the comedy of it all," he told her with a warm smile.

Clinton's smile had fallen when he followed Melissa's line of vision and spotted Remisha walking with a man who had his hand on the small of her back. Her dress complemented her curves perfectly and was short as hell!

He knew good and damn well she wasn't on a fucking date! Especially after sending him the message that she was ready for them to get back together!

Then again, it didn't matter who the dude was, he was home and back to claim her heart. The only problem was he knew if he saw her, then she saw him and with Melissa, no less. Yeah she would probably be a little upset about it at first, but once he turned on the charm and explained it away she would be putty in his hands like always. Yeah, he was going to have to stay in Cali a little longer than he originally thought.

Chapter 3

"You mentioned something about a BMW before we were interrupted, care to elaborate?" Nieko asked as soon as they were alone again, looking impressed that their drinks were now resting next to their menus. "You can count it as one of my three questions if you like," he suggested, using his straw to stir his drink.

Remisha rolled her eyes, annoyed that she even brought it up. "Uh yeah, that woman at the bar? I knew who she was the minute she spoke to you. I was pushed back into a dark memory when I saw her with him, Clinton, that's his name. Anyway, she egged and keyed my car outside of Clinton's house one night when she discovered she wasn't his one and only. Same night, I might add, I found out, too," she explained, finishing her drink and opening the menu, refusing to divulge the most heinous of Melissa's crimes.

"Interesting, so you didn't know he was seeing anyone else?" Nieko asked, already about 99.9% percent sure of her answer. Remisha did not seem like the type to be a cheater or tolerate being cheating on or used to cheat with.

"Nope, we had been together for over four years when that happened. we had just got back from a weekend in the mountains and were having dinner together before I headed home. Looking back on it now, I remember his phone blowing up all weekend but he didn't answer it and him getting a lot of 'work' texts but I didn't think anything of it at the time. About an hour after we got to his house she was pounding on the door screaming his name. He opened the door and she saw me standing in the kitchen with no shoes on, looking comfortable and at home and lost her shit. I grabbed my stuff to leave and discovered what she had done to my brand-new BMW. More than six years later it still pisses me off that she attacked my car instead of his snake ass," Remisha explained with a strained smile at the memory, still undecided on what to try for dinner.

Nieko played with the straw in his drink, watching her as she recapped what had to be a humiliating experience. He would never understand a man who found it necessary to play with one woman's emotions, let alone more than one. Because of Clinton's selfishness two women were thrown into a situation neither one wanted or deserved to be in, he had no respect for 'men' who played little boy games.

The difference between the two women seemed to be Remisha was smart enough to leave the situation, while the woman at the bar was content to continue to play and be played by Clinton.

He knew for a fact had he been a different kind of man and taken her up on her not-so-subtle offer she would have gladly left Clinton hanging for the night to spend time with him instead.

"Damn, that's all bad, Remisha, so is it safe to say you are over him?" Nieko calmly asked her again, all but sure of her answer.

"Not that it's any of your concern but yes, Nieko, I am way

over Clinton and his games," Remisha snapped, going back to her menu.

Nieko reached over and closed her menu to get her undivided attention. "Two things; first, don't play with me, Remisha, you know I am very attracted to you, so you being over him is very much my concern and second, don't ever let what another man did affect your attitude when you're with me, it's not fair to either of us and I won't tolerate it, understand?" he asked her with a soft yet stern voice. His already dark eyes shined even darker as they scanned her face.

Something about the way he was staring at her had her squirming in her seat, in most instances she would have thrown all of her attitude at him but the way Nieko called her out on her BS turned her on!

"I understand and I'm sorry for snapping at you. Neither my idiocy nor Clinton's asshole tendencies are your fault," she admitted casting a shy but lustful look across the table.

He reached over and lightly touched her face. "Another thing, the self-deprecating comments stop tonight as well. I don't like them." Nieko's voice was still stern and soft. "Now, unless I lost count, I asked three questions and now it's your turn to ask me three questions."

Remisha looked across the table again at this incredibly handsome man who so far seemed to want to care for her and make her happy and smiled, letting her guard down a little more. "Well, at the moment. I can only think of two questions. My first one being will you order for me? Because right now I'm starving and it all looks so good I can't decide and my second question, again going back to your statement about liking to play games, exactly what type of game are you trying to play with me, Nieko?" she asked twirling the last bit of her drink around to melt the ice.

Nieko's eyes flashed dark again. "All kinds of games,

Remisha and I promise you, you will like them all but know this, the difference between my games and the ones men like your ex play, is I'm playing for keeps."

"So, are we still on for lunch, Remisha?" Nieko asked her over the phone. He had invited her out to lunch the night of their first date. He told her he didn't want too much time to pass before he saw her again.

"Yes, we are. We agreed on one o'clock, right?" Remisha asked to reconfirm the time. Three days later Remisha was still floating on cloud nine from their date, his calm yet demanding demeanor was so damn sexy to her and had her wanting to know more and more about him.

"Correct, I figured I would pick you up, we'd go grab a bite to eat and go from there. Do you need to go back to the office after lunch? If so, what time do I need to have you back so I can plan accordingly?" he asked, having no idea that he was making her smile again.

His constant consideration of her time and safety was so refreshing to Remisha and a big turn on. In her history of dating no other man took the time to even ask about her time, let alone have enough sense to value it.

Remisha felt the same about him and his time as well. The other night at dinner she found out that his African gift store was almost his hobby, he was a civil engineer and ran his own company. He had such a solid team working with him that he was able to come and go as he pleased.

"Actually I came into the office pretty early to get some work done so I could take the rest of the day off once I left for lunch," Remisha answered, smiling as the receptionist walked into her office and dropped a pink handwritten message marked urgent on her desk.

She rolled her eyes heavenward when she saw who the message was from, instantly getting annoyed. *'We need to talk'* was all the message from Clinton said. Why the hell couldn't he just leave her the hell alone?

"Sounds great, I was thinking we could take a walk around Chinatown when we were done with lunch, then I will take you back to your car once we're finished walking, sound good?"

"Sounds perfect, Nieko." Remisha picked up the message slip and balled it up in her fist and tossed it into the trash can under her desk.

"Cool, see you in a few hours, beautiful," he said before he hung up.

Remisha spent several minutes after they hung up staring off into space, grinning like a damn fool.

Nieko ended his call with Remisha with a sigh and a small smile. Again his mind went back to their conversation from the other night, he learned so much about her from playing the 'three questions' game she had come up with, it was actually the perfect ice breaker.

Even before their date he could tell she'd been hurt pretty bad in a previous relationship or relationships and her general distrust of men was a direct result of those experiences.

Now having a bit more insight, he knew he was going to gently guide her into their relationship, first by gaining her trust and eventually introducing her to more about his world. She didn't know it yet but she was exactly the kind of woman he'd been looking for.

"You know what pisses me off the most, Remisha? The fact that until today you didn't bother to return even one of my phone calls or even acknowledge the gifts I sent you. It took me hinting about stopping by for you to call me today, what's up with that?" Clinton answered his phone with nothing but attitude when she returned his call.

As soon as she hung up with Nieko she called Clinton on her office phone to tell him he needed to leave her the hell alone once and for all, she was tired of his bogus attempts to pull her back into his orbit.

"Clinton, I didn't call you back because I have absolutely nothing to say to you. Now what I need you to do is stop calling my office, stop sending me gifts and just stop, period. I don't know what you thought was going to happen but it ain't happening, when I told you I was done with your ass, I meant it," Remisha told Clinton, while logging into her desktop computer to check her email, she refused to give him even an ounce more of her attention than he deserved.

"You can keep telling yourself that but you and I both know that's not true. I read your short story and I know it was me you were talking about so quit playing, girl," he told her, lowering his voice as he spoke.

Remisha swallowed back an unladylike guffaw at his failed attempt at sounding sexy. "Boy, bye! That story was exactly that, a story, make believe, not a fantasy of what I wanted you to be and damn sure not the reality of how we were! You know good and damn well you didn't support me in anything in the least so miss me with that! Shit, Lettie warned my ass that this would happen. Check your ego, Clinton, I simply gave the magazine and the readers what they wanted," Remisha told him, shaking her head, marveling at the size of the man's ego.

As far as she was concerned, 'Chocolate' was nothing more than her creative play on words. It wasn't a confession of feelings she still had for him and it most definitely wasn't an invitation for him to try and worm his way back into her heart. He needed to fade back in the shadows of the past she really wanted to forget, where he belonged.

"You're a damn good writer, Remisha, but you ain't never been that good. I just don't understand why you can't see the second chance you are asking for in that story," Clinton argued, his voice still low, he sounded like a creepy obscene phone caller.

Remisha sat back in her chair and turned over her cell phone and checked the time, Nieko would be on his way in less than three hours. She wanted to get the last ten pages she planned to work on for the day finished, and she had given Clinton more of her damn time than she wanted to, she needed to end this conversation, especially after his last snide comment.

"Whatever, Clinton, obviously my writing is that damn good, since it has you so convinced 'Chocolate' is your shady ass! You talking about second chances like you caught me cheating on you and not the other way around, and better still like I didn't see you the other night with Melissa. The fact you still even speak to that witch after what she did is mind boggling but speaks volumes about your character. Stop wasting my time, Clinton and leave me the hell alone. No more phone calls, gifts or bullshit messages, disappear!" Remisha snapped pushing the 'end call' button on her headset and putting it back on the base to charge.

She stood up and let out a frustrated sigh before moving back to her bean bag to attempt to finish her work, knowing she was about to see Nieko again already had her hormones humming.

Clinton ran his hand down his face in frustration after Remisha hung up on him, he understood she was a little upset about seeing him with Melissa but she had to know it wasn't that damn serious. Besides, he had bought her flowers and gifts to make up for it and to not even acknowledge them was just plain rude, so he had more of a right to be upset than she did.

Yeah, they needed to talk sooner rather than later so he was going to have to do a pop up.

Clinton drove to her office and pulled up next to the car he now knew was hers, he followed her home from San Diego a couple weeks ago because he had to keep tabs on his girl. Once he saw the delivery man go inside with his latest gift, he opened up the door to get out of his car when he saw the big dude Remisha was with the other night walking into her office building.

"Ain't this about a bitch?" he snapped, slamming his car door closed again. Yeah they needed to have a talk in private ASAP, he was tired of her playing with his emotions!

"Remisha, you have a guest at the front desk, should I send him back or have him wait here for you?" The part time receptionist Liza asked over her intercom, exactly three hours later. She was an older woman who came in a few times a week to cover when Elisha, who also happened to be pregnant but further along than Letecia, went to her appointments.

Remisha had finally been able to become so engrossed in the story she was working on, that she lost track of time. Her initial plan had been to freshen up her light makeup before he got there but too late now.

"Go ahead and send him back, please and thank you, Liza," Remisha answered, uncurling her legs from under her, standing up and stretching her arms over her head.

A few seconds later the knock at her office door had her stomach jumping nervously as she crossed the room to open it.

"Good afternoon, Remisha. I have to say you look as beautiful as always," Nieko said as soon as he stepped into her office handing her a stargazer lily.

Remisha accepted the flower blinking and smiling like an idiot. Nieko was dressed in slacks and a short-sleeve polo, his hair had been freshly cut and edged up, his mustache was trimmed. With the handsome smile plastered on his face, he looked absolutely edible.

"Thank you, you're sweet to say that but I lost track of time and I know I look a mess," Remisha answered nervously touching her hair and looking down at her black, silk slipper covered feet.

Nieko was in front of her in a flash, lightly grasping her chin making her look up at him. "I thought I made myself clear the other night when I said all self-deprecating comments had come to an end?" His eyes were dark as he looked deeply into her eyes. "As you get to know me, Remisha you will come to learn I don't like to repeat myself and what happens when I'm forced to. You are a beautiful woman period, and you are never to explain away my compliments but simply accept them," he ordered and tilted her head back a little further and pressed his lips to hers briefly before letting her chin go and taking a step back.

"Noted, give me a minute to wrap up here and I'll be ready to go?" she asked, sliding her laptop into her bag along with her wallet and phone. Her lips tingled from his soft kiss and she felt herself blush and flash hot as she wondered what *would* happen when he was forced to repeat himself. She was once again surprised by her reaction to his forceful demeanor.

"Sure take your time, I didn't make reservations anywhere this time. I just figured we would wander around and find something along the way especially since you said you don't have to be back here today," Nieko explained, settling into one of the chairs in her office closest to the door.

Nieko knew he surprised her with his flash of temper but the sooner she knew what he was about, the better. Nothing set him off quicker than self-depreciation, he felt that everyone needed to be their own biggest supporter, that's why it was called 'self' esteem. Besides explaining away his compliments implied he was being insincere when he gave them, which was never the case.

He could still taste her on his lips and knew it was only because of his willpower that their very brief kiss didn't go any further. Even though they had only been out twice he knew they needed to talk before they went any further, his hormones were pushing up his normal time table.

Nieko watched her quietly as she sat down in front of her desktop, her fingers flew across her wireless keyboard for a few minutes before she clicked the mouse and logged out and hoped she was as open minded as she seemed, not that it mattered, because he had already decided, one way or another Remisha was going to be completely his.

"So tell me again what you don't like to eat in Chinese food?" Remisha asked, covering her teasing smile with her napkin while sitting across the table from Nieko who had apparently just bit into the tiniest piece of baby corn. She thought she had picked out all of the offending vegetable from their fried rice but it appeared she missed a small piece.

"I already told you, Remisha, that shit is so nasty!" he grumbled with a frown wiping his mouth.

On the drive over, they were enjoying each other's company so much that instead of eating first they opted to walk around first and have a late lunch/early dinner in Chinatown.

Remisha took another bite of the fried rice they were sharing and watched Nieko, whose face was serious, as he sifted through his portion of their rice with his chopsticks making sure there were no more pieces of baby corn.

She'd noticed everything he did was done with that same meticulous attention to detail. Even when it started to rain a little, he knew exactly where to go to grab an umbrella to keep them dry.

Nieko was nothing like any man she had ever dated. She already loved his sense of humor and the laid back, easy going demeanor he had most of the time and his flashes of temper did something to her psyche and libido

"What are you thinking about?" Nieko asked, bringing her out of her musing. His eyes were sparkling and low, a playful smile on his face as he looked at her.

Remisha sighed moving the food around her plate with her chopsticks debating if she should tell him where her thoughts were. "Honestly, I was thinking about what a good time I'm having with you, Nieko," she heard herself say, this man and his intense dark eyes were like truth serum, she didn't think she could withhold information from him even if she wanted to!

Nieko set his chopsticks aside and reached over the table taking her hand in his. "That's a good thing and I'm glad to hear that, Remisha, I'm enjoying your company as well. I hope that means we can continue to see each other?" Nieko asked, leaning forward and dropping soft kisses on the back of her hand.

Remisha crossed her legs tight in an attempt to quiet her awakening middle, damn this man and his wonderful lips! "Oh most definitely, Nieko. I haven't had this much fun in a very long time," Remisha told him, picking up and taking a sip of her green tea to ward off the chill from the rain outside.

Nieko stared across at her still holding her hand, his mind was flipping through 1001 questions he wanted to ask but settled on the simple and most nagging one, "Can I expect exclusivity while we are doing this, Remisha or do you have other hearts you plan on stringing along?" he asked seriously, never one to share his attention once he was pursuing someone. He expected the same amount of respect and loyalty from the woman he was focused on.

Remisha sipped more of her tea and slipped her hand from him and sighed giving him a deadpan look. "Come on now, Nieko, that's kind of a silly question to ask at this point isn't it?"

He picked up his chopsticks again and regarded her with an arched eyebrow. "Silly or not, it's one I expect you to answer," he told her, putting a healthy bite of chicken and rice into his mouth.

"If I'm seeing you, then I am only seeing you, Nieko. I haven't joined the circus lately and I have no interest in learning how to juggle," she told him matter of factly.

Nieko chuckled at her remark about the circus, Remisha and her smart mouth would most definitely keep him on his toes. "Good to know and where do you want to see this thing between us go?" he asked, moving his chopsticks through the Mongolian beef looking at her again.

"Nieko, I have no idea. I just usually go with the flow and see where it leads, what about you?" Remisha asked, squirming under his intense gaze.

"My hopes are we are headed towards a relationship, a particular type of relationship," he informed her, taking what he decided was his last bite of food.

Remisha poured more green tea, thinking about what he said. "What type of relationship are you hoping to have with me, Nieko?"

To her dismay, he lifted his hand to get their server's attention and asked for their check. She was finished eating but she wasn't ready for their date to end.

"Let's table that discussion for another day in the very near future, Remisha, just be reassured your happiness and safety will continue to be a priority for me," he told her cryptically with a sexy wink. "Did you save room for dessert? I know a pretty good ice cream spot not too far from here, I figured we could grab some and continue our conversation, maybe even walk around a little more?" Nieko suggested, signing the credit card slip their server had presented him with after running his card.

"Sounds good, but you do realize it's still raining right?" Remisha asked pointing to the window behind him and the falling rain outside.

Nieko stood and helped her from her side of the booth, bringing her close to him, he touched her face before leaning down and kissing her softly.

"No worries, beautiful, you might get a little wet, but I promise I'll keep you warm."

"Lettie, I'm telling you, girl, that man is almost too good to be true! He opens doors and pulls out chairs for me and everything, and did I tell you he brings me a different flower at the beginning of every date we go on? I even messed around and gave his ass my address!" Remisha revealed to Letecia a month later when she went down to San Diego at Brent's request. They were in the waiting room for Letecia's appointment, she drove down to go with Letecia because Brent was out of town.

"Oh shit! Nieko knows the location of 'The Dollhouse'? Yeah, you must really be feeling him, and your evil ass didn't want to call him! See what you were missing out on? Sometimes trusting your best friend is all you need to do and I take my apologies in the form of cookies, lavender butter cookies to be exact." Letecia smirked, smiling at Remisha who had been talking her ear off about Nieko since she picked her up forty-five minutes ago, like she didn't call and talk about him every night since their first date anyway.

Letecia lovingly called Remisha's house 'The Dollhouse' because it reminded her of the dollhouse they played with as little girls back home in Alabama.

"Yeah, yeah, Lettie I'm sorry I fussed at you for inviting him to sit at our table and I will gladly make your butter cookies when I come down for the weekend next Friday."

Letecia laid her head on Remisha's shoulder and batted her eyelashes. "But you're here today, Remy and me and your god baby or god babies really really need them," she begged, with a pout.

"Not happening, I have plans tonight and sweating in your hot ass kitchen is not part of them," Remisha told her, pushing Letecia's head off of her shoulder.

"Remy, please, now that I know I'm going to be home all alone all weekend, it would be so much easier to face knowing I have fresh baked cookies." Letecia grabbed her by the shoulders shaking her playfully until one of the medical assistants called her name to take her back for her appointment.

"This guilt trip isn't over, Remy," Letecia warned Remisha and motioned for her to go back with her.

Remisha pulled up in her garage three hours later, her face hurting from smiling so much. It was official, Letecia was having triplets! They weren't due for another five and half months but her best friend was about to be a mommy of three! Remisha was so happy Brent was able to be Facetimed in to see them too. The tears of joy both shared warmed her heart, she was so happy for them and even though it cut her timetable pretty much in half, she baked Letecia her damn butter cookies before she headed back to Los Angeles.

Stepping into her house she rushed upstairs to figure out what she was going to wear on her date with Nieko when her phone vibrated in her purse. Four missed calls from Nieko, shit! She not only forgot to turn her ringer back on after Letecia's appointment but she forgot to text him to tell him she was on her way back, yeah she was about to hear it.

After debating on calling him back, Remisha decided to wait for the tongue lashing she knew she was in for, and to at least look sexy and tempting as hell when she got it.

"Who the hell?" Remisha muttered with a frown. She was pushing one of her white gold, infinity symbol, dangle earrings in her earlobe when the doorbell sounded, way too early to be Nieko. Must have the wrong house, she decided and went back to getting ready.

She finished putting her earrings on and stepped into her four-inch heels checking her reflection in her full-length mirror. The plum-colored wrap around dress hugged her curves perfectly and gave her just the right amount of cleavage. Remisha wore her hair down in natural curls, the way it was styled brought focus to her face especially her dark plum lipstick hued lips.

She was moving her wallet and keys to her smaller bag when the doorbell sounded again, twice in rapid succession.

"Who the hell is at my damn door?" she muttered, rushing down the stairs to her front door.

Clinton stood on her porch with a huge smile on his face, holding a bouquet of roses out to her.

"What in the fresh hell, Clinton? Why the fuck are you at my house?" Remisha demanded checking the time, Nieko was due there in twenty minutes, which in Nieko time meant he would be pulling up in about ten. She needed this idiot gone like yesterday.

"I wanted to finish our conversation in person, but it looks like you have plans. Where the hell do you think you're going in a dress like that?" he demanded, walking inside of her foyer uninvited.

"Not that it is any of your damn business, but yes I do have plans and what conversation, Clinton? I said all I needed to say to your bothersome ass a month ago, now leave," she demanded with her hands on her hips.

"Remy, we are nowhere near finished talking and you still haven't answered my question, where the hell do you think you're going in that dress? I know we have a lot to hash out and until then you are pretty much single but nah I gotta draw the line somewhere, that dress is out," he told her looking her up and down like he owned her or something. "So go change and name a date and time we can have an uninterrupted conversation," he requested reaching out, moving a curl away from her face.

Remisha slapped his hand away angrily. "Where I am going and what I am wearing is none of your goddamn business and I ain't changing shit! Dafuq you thought! Furthermore, don't touch me and my name is Remisha to you, not Remy and I want you to take you and your pitiful ass flowers the *fuck* outta my house now!" Remisha snapped, feeling her face getting hot with anger. The nerve of this idiot showing up unannounced at her house giving her orders and shit!

"Not until you stop playing this silly game of yours and agree to meet me for lunch so we can talk," Clinton told her while trying to hand her the flowers again.

"Did you fall and hit your head or something, recently? This is not a game! I don't like your ass and I don't want anything and I do mean *anything* to do with you, now *leave*!" Remisha yelled, feeling herself about to lose her shit.

Clinton seemed unmoved by her fit of temper and was about to say something when someone cleared their throat behind him. No, not someone, Nieko.

"Now, that's twice I've heard her ask you to leave, the next request won't be coming from her and believe me I am nowhere near as polite as the lovely Remisha is," Nieko told Clinton, walking past him, turning and standing facing him with his back to Remisha.

Nieko's demeanor appeared calm but knowing him for the last month or so she could tell he was pissed.

Clinton gave Nieko a hostile glare before smirking at him and dropping the roses on the table near her front door and storming out of her house.

Nieko followed Clinton to the door, closing and locking it behind him. She could feel the barely controlled anger rolling off of him in her small foyer.

"Nieko, I'm sorry about that. I promise you I didn't invite him here, he just showed up and I told him over a month ago I didn't want–" Remisha started to explain when Nieko turned around, his dark eyes flashing angrily, stopping her in her tracks.

"He is not, nor will he ever be, my concern. My concern is you and your wellbeing. If I remember correctly, I asked you to call me when you got to Leticia's and when you were on your way back home and neither happened." Nieko took her by the hand and led her back to her living room.

"Yes, you did, and I'm sorry. I honestly forgot. I was so

excited to find out about the bab–" Remisha began to explain when Nieko cut her off again by lightly touching her lips with his finger.

"None of that matters, beautiful. The bottom line is I made a request and you failed to honor it," he told her matter of factly, sitting on the couch and having her sit next to him. His voice was calm and patient but his dark eyes were flashing impatiently.

Remisha didn't know what to expect or how to feel at this point she had never seen him like this before. It had her both intrigued and nervous at the same time.

"As lovely as you look tonight, regrettably I believe we should stay in. I think it's time to have a conversation about what type of relationship I want to have with you and all that it entails," he said, as he pulled out his phone and dialed a number. She sat next to him quietly as he cancelled their reservation for dinner. When he finished he looked at her thoughtfully.

"Now, I'm sure by now you can tell I am a man who likes to lead. I like it in all aspects of my life and especially my relationships." Nieko silenced his phone and placed it on her coffee table in front of the couch.

Remisha looked down at her hands that were folded in her lap, not sure how she felt about what he just said. She was way too independent to be led or controlled by anyone. No matter how attracted she was to Nieko, she wasn't having it. "I don't want to be controlled, Nieko. As a matter of fact, I won't be controlled," she stated firmly, feeling sad that their budding relationship was most likely coming to an end.

Nieko used his finger to lift her chin and make her look at him. "Indulge me for a few minutes before you start overthinking this, okay?" he asked her with a small smile. He waited until Remisha nodded in agreement before continuing.

"Let me ask you this, Remisha. The entire time we've been seeing each other have you ever felt controlled or like you didn't have a voice in anything?" he asked her, touching her face again with the same small smile.

Remisha thought about it and she realized she never felt controlled or railroaded. As a matter of fact, Nieko always made her feel cherished, and beautiful, and like he genuinely cared about her.

"No, never, Nieko. You have always asked for my opinion and input on what we did or where we went unless you had a surprise or something very specific planned. But we are not talking about how things have been so far, but how you want us to progress from here on out, correct?" she asked with a sigh, slipping her feet out of her heels and folding her legs under her bottom on the couch.

"Remisha, our relationship would continue just as it is now with certain expectations and a clearer understanding of what I expect of you," Nieko explained, looking into her eyes. His eyes appeared calmer than they did a few minutes before.

Again Remisha felt herself becoming defensive. "Exactly what would you expect of me, Nieko?" she asked folding her arms, her eyes narrowing suspiciously.

"First and foremost, flashes of attitude like that will not be tolerated. I will not be disrespected, ever." He reached over and unfolded her arms. "You can express how you feel in more respectful ways, Remisha," he said firmly, taking her hand and running his thumb over the top of it.

"I'm sorry you feel disrespected, but so do I, Nieko. I'm almost feeling like the way I am is not good enough for you," Remisha explained as politely as she could with the way she was feeling.

"Bear with me, everything will be clear in a few minutes. And, for the record, that last comment was a little self-deprecating but I will let it slide considering the fact you don't know all of the details of what I'm asking of you just yet. First of all, I wouldn't be sitting here talking about any of this if I wasn't very interested in you. Never doubt my attraction for you, I know you feel it as much as I do. That being said, I expect you to behave a certain way at all times, honor my requests, never be disrespectful in any way and if, or when, you break those rules, there will be consequences. In return, I will love you, cherish you, and protect you," Nieko explained carefully, still looking deeply into her eyes.

Despite the seriousness of their conversation, the way he was looking at her made her insides jump excitedly as she wondered what those consequences might be. "What kind of consequences?" she asked with a small smile of her own.

"Well, considering you ignored my requests and then my phone calls earlier, I can show you better than I can tell you," he said, dropping her hand and unbuttoning the cuff of his sleeves before he started to roll them up.

Remisha looked nervously over at him as he rolled up his sleeves with a no nonsense look on his face.

"Do you trust me, Remisha?" he asked, rising to his feet before helping her to stand as well.

Nieko watched her nervously shift her weight from one foot to the other for several seconds before she took a deep breath and nodded. "Yes, I trust you, Nieko," she said softly, looking up at him with curious eyes.

"The lifestyle is called Domestic Discipline. When you are disrespectful, don't follow the rules, or don't honor my wishes, you will be disciplined. Do you understand what that means? Are you willing to allow me to do this?" he asked, taking both of her hands in his.

He saw a hint of hesitation move across her face before she looked down at her feet, shaking her head in the negative. "It means you want to hit me, right? I'm not feeling that, Nieko," she said sadly, pulling her hands back, looking at her feet, and taking a step back from him.

Nieko moved forward closing the small gap her step backwards created, taking her hands again. "Look at me, Remisha," he ordered with a soft voice. He figured she would react this way but he was also sure she would come around to his way of thinking the more he broke things down for her.

Remisha sighed and looked at him with tears in her eyes. "I have really been having a good time with you, but I'm not going to agree to be abused," she told him, shaking her head sadly.

"Of course you're not, nor would I ask you to. I am talking about light spankings, corner time, writing lines, or similar things, Remisha, not abuse. I wouldn't do anything we hadn't already agreed upon. I know this sounds kind of strange and even a little scary, but a moment ago you said you trusted me, do you trust me enough to show you what domestic discipline would be like?" Nieko asked her, moving even closer to her.

Remisha bit the corner of her bottom lip nervously, looking at him with a small frown. "Why do you want this with me? What do you get out of this?" she asked him.

"I honestly believe it's a relationship you will enjoy being a part of and I'm not the only one who benefits from this kind of relationship. You do, too as I explained. I get the satisfaction of guiding and leading you, knowing you will do what is necessary to keep yourself safe and healthy, carry yourself in a respectable way, all the things you already do for the most part even when I'm not around makes me happy and turns me on. Just like I have you mind, body and soul, you have me, too. Our relationship will change between us and become stronger and will include discipline. Now I have to ask you again, do you trust me enough to show you what my discipline is like?" Nieko asked her, pressing his forehead to hers.

Remisha stepped back and grabbed him on both sides of

his face, forcing him to look her in the eyes. "Okay, I'm curious enough to see what this is all about but you have to promise me if I ask you to stop, then you stop, agreed?" she asked him, her eyes bored into his.

Nieko smiled down at her excitedly. "Agreed, we can even pick a safe word if you like."

Chapter 4

"Safe word?" she asked curiously. The truly wicked grin that spread across Nieko's face almost had Remisha rethinking what she just agreed to.

He walked her over to one end of the couch in her living room. He pushed on the arm to make sure it was stable and not too hard before positioning her over it.

"Now, Remisha, you are aware of why you're being disciplined, correct?" he asked, his eyes dark and serious.

Remisha nodded and shrugged her shoulders. "I guess so," she answered with a frown.

Without warning, Nieko smacked her on her ass. Remisha yelped, rubbing her stinging buttcheek. New sensations began to swirl between her legs.

"When I ask you a direct question, I expect a direct answer. You already know I don't like repeating myself. Now, answer me," Nieko demanded, repositioning her so her bottom was on top of the couch arm and her upper body lay comfortably on the couch cushion, he moved her dress up, exposing her thong and bare ass cheeks.

Remisha blinked and swallowed fearfully as he lightly

rubbed her bottom while standing directly behind her. "Because you told me to call you to let you know I made it to Letecia's safely and also when I was on my way back and I didn't. I didn't answer my phone or return your calls either," Remisha confessed, barely above a whisper.

Nieko moved her feet apart and stepped between her spread legs and leaned forward until his front was resting on her back, his weight braced on his arms on either side of her as he whispered in her ear, "Exactly, but don't get shy on me now, Remisha. You did that shit, so own that shit!" he hissed in her ear catching her earlobe between his teeth before standing back up and smacking her a little harder on both cheeks.

Remisha's breath caught in her chest as the sting moved through her body making her moan involuntarily. What the fuck was wrong with her? This shouldn't be turning her on but she felt her clit beginning to flutter and pulse in response.

"I just forgot about the not returning my calls part just that quick," Nieko said thoughtfully before bringing his hand down on her ass again, a bit harder than he did the first three times. "Do you have any idea how worried I was about you?" he asked. "You're getting ten smacks on this lovely ass of yours for the ten hours of worry you caused me."

Remisha's eyes popped open in fear. "Ten?" she asked, trying to stand upright and look at him.

Nieko pressed her back down on the couch. "Ten, you're going to count them out loud and if you stand up we will start over," he instructed sternly, moving his hand across her right buttcheek, and knowing he wouldn't be adding any more force than he was already using. She wouldn't know that though, because with each smack the heat was going to continue to build.

Remisha felt his hand leave her ass and swiftly come back in contact with a smack that sent chills down her spine.

Nieko paused watching her reaction, she gripped the cushion of the couch tightly and quietly whispered, "One."

He brought his hand down on the same cheek again. "I told you to own that shit!" he growled down at her.

"Shit! Two!" Remisha counted louder through clenched teeth, her pussy quivered as her excitement grew.

Nieko smiled wickedly bringing his hand down on Remisha's ample ass over and over again, if only she could see how sexy she looked in this position, moaning and squirming as she counted. He kept count with her to keep his own arousal under control, his time would come, right now this was all about her.

"Ten!" Remisha panted with her eyes closed tight with some tears escaping, her ass was on fire and her entire body tingled with desire. Her thighs were wet with her juices. She had never been so turned on in her entire life.

Nieko helped her stand upright, his labored breathing caused his chest to rise and fall as he pulled her to him and held her tight.

"How are you feeling? I'm proud of you, you took your spanking well," he whispered in her ear, he could feel her shivering in his arms. His mouth moved from her ear and down the length of her neck.

"I'm okay and I'm sorry for my behavior," Remisha answered feeling lighter and also like she was about to explode. She wanted Nieko so bad, it hurt! She had no idea what was going on with her or why being disciplined turned her on so much but her nipples were erect and pressed against the material of her dress, her thong was sopping wet, her clit was swollen and sending waves of need through her. She closed her eyes and moaned loudly in frustration when he moved his head from her neck to look down at her.

"What's the matter, beautiful?" he asked her with a knowing grin, he moved his hand slowly down her body, purposely brushing his hand across one of her erect nipples as he went, he moved his hands underneath her dress and touched her pussy lightly over her thong.

She moved her legs apart giving him better access to her middle, silently begging him to touch her, another moan escaping her lips.

"Just so you know, discipline is usually not followed by sex." He could have sworn he heard her growl. He knew she'd react like this and he couldn't be happier. "I may make an exception since this is your first time and you were a good girl. Use your words, tell me exactly what you want," he whispered, his hand was still cupping her thong covered middle, she saw his erection beginning to grow as he used his middle finger to move the flimsy material of her thong to the side before sliding it into her quivering wetness.

He leaned down and captured her lips in a fiery kiss, pushing his tongue deep inside her inviting mouth. Nieko began to move his finger in and out of her a few times causing her knees to buckle.

"I want you, Nieko. I want you to take me out of this damn dress, I want you to touch and kiss me all over. I want you to do whatever you've been wanting to do to me since you met me. I need you to fuck me and make love to me at the same time. I want you to put out this fire you caused that's swirling around inside of me right now," Remisha boldly told Nieko, still moaning, her eyes fluttering open and closed as he fingered her pussy.

"Mmm, all of that, huh?" he moaned against her lips before kissing her again. "Consider it done, beautiful," he promised, pushing a second finger inside of her, increasing the tempo of his hand while keeping her cradled tight in the crook of his arm.

Nieko moved his fingers in and out of Remisha's treasure swiftly, her moans filling the air around them. She had her arms locked around his neck as she rode his fingers, her eyes were closed tight, her bottom lip caught between her teeth. To Nieko she was the perfect picture of arousal.

He moved his lips, lightly biting her neck causing her to shiver. He moved his mouth against her ear. "Let go, Remisha, come for me," he demanded with a low growl.

Remisha's breath picked up to a panting pace as her vaginal walls squeezed and quaked around his moving fingers. "No, not this way, I don't want it to be over," she begged and whined as Nieko's fingers pulled a shuddering orgasm from her.

His fingers continued to move in and out of her until her contracting vagina stilled around his fingers and her heavy breathing was reduced to a contented sigh.

"I gave you what you earned and needed, but I promise you there is more to come," he whispered with his mouth still pressed against her ear, pulling his dripping, wet fingers from her center.

Nieko made sure she was steady on her feet and quickly removed her thong and dress, she wasn't wearing a bra. When she was standing in front of him completely nude, he grabbed her by the back of her head and pushed his tongue deep inside her mouth and walked her backwards to the couch.

Nieko's mouth moved all over her body, while he came out of his button-down shirt. Once he was finished, his hands joined his mouth tasting and touching her all over.

Watching her come had sent his hormones into overdrive,

he grabbed her breast aggressively and clamped his mouth on the nipple, sucking hard. His erection was tenting his pants as he pushed her down on the couch.

"Fuck, I want you, Remisha." He recaptured her lips, her tongue was just as aggressive as his this time.

To his surprise, she reached up and undid his belt, unfastened his pants and pushed them and his underwear down over his hips and eagerly grabbed his erection, moving her hand up and down his hard smoothness.

Her tongue moved around inside of his mouth rolling and tumbling with his, as animalistic sounds and moans continued to rise from her body. He moved his hand back between her legs and found her even wetter than he left her minutes before. She arched her back moaning louder when he pushed his fingers back inside her pussy.

Remisha pulled her lips from his and leaned forward kissing his chest. Her lips began their descent down his body until she paused with her mouth just above the head of his dick. "Have I told you how much I love chocolate, better yet, let me show you," she whispered looking up at him seductively before swallowing his entire length. Nieko's hands dropped to his sides as his eyes rolled back in his head in pleasure.

Remisha moaned blissfully as Nieko's erection slid in and out of her mouth, she repositioned herself to move her head more freely as she took him deep in her mouth several times before moving her head back until only the tip remained in her mouth and swirled her tongue around the head while her hand jacked him off.

Nieko was still on his feet, he was leaning over Remisha with his hands gripping the couch behind her to maintain his balance as he watched his dick disappear in and out of her mouth. "Damn, baby," he moaned, throwing his head back.

She savored the taste of him as he tentatively began to move his hips back and forward pushing himself deeper into her suctioning mouth. The look of pleasure on his face, with his eyes closed and head thrown back turned her on even more.

Every part of her body was singing, the flames of desire were burning her from the inside out, she fought to ignore her own feelings of need as she treated Nieko to her warm mouth. When she swallowed his length whole again and used her hand to massage his balls she felt the muscles in his legs tense up.

"Yes, baby, swallow that dick," Nieko moaned, grabbing her by the back of her head thrusting in and out of her mouth with more force.

Remisha grabbed him by the side of his muscular thighs and angled her mouth so she was directly in front of him and his thrust went even deeper inside her mouth, she was in her zone.

She loved the sound of Nieko's moans as he moved in and out of her mouth, the sounds of surprise he made as he went deeper inside her mouth, only to realize she didn't have a gag reflex, made her open her mouth wider and swallow more of him.

He moaned even louder, pulling her head back by her hair until only the tip of his dick was in her mouth as he looked down at her through lowered lids, breathing hard, looking like he was fighting to regain control.

She looked up at him seductively as she gripped his erection tight and sucked hard on the tip of his dick before pushing her tongue inside the hole on his helmet, tasting his precum. The way he was looking down at her with her hair gripped in his tight fist was taking over the edge of self-control.

She could tell by the way his butt cheeks clenched that he

wanted to drive himself deep inside of her mouth again. With her eyes still on his, she slowly ran her tongue down the length of his hard shaft and around his balls and up the other side before taking him in her mouth again with a deep moan, making the decision for him.

He grabbed handfuls of her hair in both of his hands and began to fuck her mouth like a mad man. The veins in his dick pulsated and vibrated on her tongue as the helmet grew large and engorged.

Remisha sucked harder, allowing him to go as deep as he could inside of her mouth, she felt him jerk forward as he began to come. His muscular legs locked underneath her tight grip as he released his warm load inside her mouth and down her throat.

"Fuck, Remisha! Shit! Girl!" he yelled, his hands were still pulling her hair while he continued to come. Remisha sucked and swallowed until she was sure he was finished coming and sat back on the couch, letting his semi-hard, still twitching penis fall from her mouth.

Nieko collapsed on the couch next to her, pulling his pants and underwear completely off, tossing them to the side. "You know that wasn't even right, Remisha, you could have warned me or something," he told her, still trying to catch his breath.

Remisha looked at him with a small smile. "Yeah and you could have told me or warned me too! Got me over here climbing walls and shit after my 'discipline'!" she countered back.

Nieko's wicked grin had returned. "So I take it you enjoyed being disciplined?" he asked her, grabbing one of her hands and pulling her into his arms.

"It wasn't at all how I thought it would be, honestly. I don't know what I was expecting but definitely not how I reacted to it," she admitted, closing her eyes and laying her head on his chest.

"So is it safe to say you're willing to give our relationship a try?" Nieko asked, lifting her head by her chin so she was looking at him.

"Nieko, I need you to be patient with me. This will be an adjustment for me and if you're willing to do that, then I'm willing to give this kind of a relationship a try. I hope you understand my reservations."

"As I said before only certain aspects of our relationship change, the general foundation we have already built remains the same," Nieko told her, leaning forward and capturing her lips in a kiss again. "I had plans to devour your sexy ass tonight but I have to admit after that amazing and very surprising display of skill on your part, I'm in serious need of sustenance to refuel first," he admitted, grabbing his phone to order them dinner.

"So what time are you driving out?" Nieko asked Remisha a week and a day later, pulling her into his arms at his house. She was heading back to San Diego to spend the weekend with Letecia.

He'd noticed her car was making a whining noise and told her to bring it to his house before she left. While he'd worked on her car, she cooked them a late lunch and was working on her own final edits for her next freelance short story until he was done..

"I was planning to head out around three-thirty or four this afternoon at the latest, you requested I leave before it starts to get dark so I figured that would be an acceptable time?" Remisha asked, putting her arms around his neck. "Did you figure out what the noise was?"

After their relationship talk at her house the other night, Remisha had learned when Nieko *requested* something it meant that was what he expected her to do. Much to her relief, just like he said, not much had really changed between them and while they still hadn't picked up where they left off the other day, she was more than satisfied with the way things were going so far.

"Yeah, it's your serpentine belt so you're going to take my car to Letecia's and I will have your car ready by the time you get back," he instructed, kissing her on the forehead before washing his hands in the kitchen sink, so they could eat.

Remisha opened her mouth to protest and ask what he was going to do for transportation all weekend when he looked at her over his shoulder with his eyebrow arched expectantly.

Her mouth snapped closed. Even though being disciplined turned her on immensely, she was finally able to sit down without a stinging reminder.

"Okay sounds like a plan," she answered, before starting to hum and move to plate their food.

Nieko swallowed back a laugh, drying his hands. "Good save, beautiful." He smirked, smacking her on the ass as she walked by. "I see you found something to cook for lunch too." He watched her with his arms folded leaning on the counter near the sink.

Remisha yelped, her eyes narrowing but she paused to check her facial expression before turning around to face him again.

"Uh, yeah, I found some crabmeat in the freezer so I made crab salad in avocados and a simple pasta carbonara." She walked over to the small kitchen table and set the plates of food down on it.

Just like the last time, she was already getting wet but she knew they really didn't have time to get into anything before she left for San Diego. Besides, she didn't want to want him right now, the bastard!

"So, my baby is very creative in the kitchen I see. You'll

find that I am too but in a very different way, of course," he bragged, looking impressed as he sat down to eat.

"I can only imagine," Remisha quipped, wanting badly to rub her stinging buttcheek. She pulled a bottle of white wine out of his fridge and two glasses from the glass rack suspended above his kitchen island. She took two steps towards the table and saw him watching her thoughtfully, his eyes moving to the bottle of wine which she quickly exchanged with peach flavored sparkling water with a disgruntled look she tried to hide as a smirk.

Nieko took the glasses and the bottle from her and poured them each a glass of sparkling water with a look of amusement still on his face. "You'll find out sooner rather than later if you keep that attitude up," he threatened as she sat down across from him.

Remisha's middle jumped, she was more than curious to find out about Nieko's *talents* in the kitchen. The little devil on her shoulder was telling her there was no time like the present to find out more about them, trip or no trip.

"I don't have an attitude, Nieko and didn't do anything to get smacked on the ass for either," she snapped, biting the inside of her cheek to keep from smiling, then picked up her fork and took a bite of food before looking over at him.

He sighed with a shake of his head and went back to eating his lunch, not saying a word. Every time she looked up from her plate his dark eyes were watching her, his jaw working even when he stopped chewing.

When they were finished eating, Remisha got up from the table and went to pick up his plate and take it to the kitchen with hers. She was kind of disappointed he didn't react the way she expected him to when he reached out suddenly and grabbed her arm.

"Change of plans, call Letecia and let her know you might get there a little later than normal. I'm driving you up after you and I have a little *talk*," he informed her, his voice was low and menacing before he let her go and stood up leaving the kitchen.

"Oh fuck," she whispered to herself as she pulled out her phone to call Letecia.

Nieko casually leaned on the doorframe of the kitchen after he showered and changed into a comfortable pair of sweats and a tank top. Remisha was sitting at his kitchen island on her laptop.

Her fingers were flying across her keyboard and she jumped in surprise when she looked up and noticed him there silently watching her. "I-uh- I told Lettie I would be there around seven or so and she told me to tell you 'Hi'," she said nervously, watching him when he moved further into the kitchen and quietly started grabbing things from the cabinet closest to the garage and then his walk-in pantry.

"Are you about finished?" he asked her, indicating her open laptop, completely ignoring what she said about Letecia. He took everything he grabbed from the kitchen to his bedroom, and just like he expected, by the time he came back into the kitchen, her laptop was out of sight.

"Excellent, so let's talk about your attitude, shall we?" he asked leaning over the bar directly in front of her, his eyes boring into hers, extending his hand.

He saw the look of fear that leapt into her eyes before it was replaced by curious excitement as she stepped down from the high bar chair taking his hand. Nieko silently walked her through his house and to his room, the black bedspread on his bed was folded down to the foot of the bed exposing crisp white sheets. He had a credenza against the wall next to the bed, she could see the items he took from the kitchen neatly laid out along with a few things she couldn't identify.

"Remisha, I had every intention of taking things slow with you, but you insist on pushing your luck so I believe a little learning game is in order before you go away for the weekend," Nieko announced touching her face lightly, he could already feel his dick stirring at the thought of what he was about to do to her.

"A learning game?" Remisha asked, looking up at him anxiously. He noticed her nipples were erect under her t-shirt.

"Yeah, a learning game. I call it pleasure and pain. I mean, it's what you and that smart ass mouth and attitude wanted, right? That's the only reason I can think of for you being so defiant at lunch," Nieko stated, his face emotionless, again he saw fear leap into her eyes only to be taken over by curiosity a split second later.

"Before we begin I want you to choose a safe word, 'stop', 'no', and 'don't' are not an option. I'm warning you now, they will be ignored no matter how loud you scream them and believe me, you are about to scream them all, Remisha."

Nieko moved and sat down on the side of his bed and had Remisha stand between his legs. Reaching up he untucked her t-shirt and pulled it over her head tossing it aside. "So think of a word you wouldn't utter in the screams of passion, and remember when you say that word, everything stops immediately so be sure you mean what you say and say what you mean," He instructed unfastening her jean shorts and pushing them over her hips and off.

Nieko licked his lips staring at her lace covered pussy directly in front of his face. Part of him wanted to bury his face deep in her sweet spot right now, but all in due time, so he settled for leaning forward and placing a warm kiss there instead.

He walked over to the credenza and picked up a blindfold

and noise cancelling headphones and brought them back to where Remisha was standing.

He moved behind her and tied the blindfold in place and put the behind the neck headphones around her neck with the wired earbuds in one of her ears. He was a little surprised she hadn't protested at all. He ground his growing erection against her ass and whispered in her ear, "What's the word, Remisha?" He chuckled against her ear when she shivered and broke out in goose bumps.

Remisha swallowed hard, opening and closing her mouth nervously several times, her hands were gripped tight together in front of her, and she took a deep breath. "Chocolate," she said bravely, dropping her hands to her sides and standing tall.

If she was able to see the evil smile that moved across Nieko's face at that moment, Remisha would have run the hell out of his house only wearing her underwear and shoes.

"Got it. Game on," he growled and pushed the other earbud into her ear.

Remisha's heart slammed against her ribs as she stood in complete silence and darkness not knowing what to expect, her braveness from a few moments ago completely gone.

She almost jumped out of her skin when she felt Nieko lift one foot then the other to take off her leather flats, he dragged his hands up her legs slowly and removed her thong and her bra soon followed.

Next she felt herself being guided somewhere, she let out a sigh of relief when he helped her climb up on the bed, for a split second she thought maybe he was going to chain her to a wall or something. Once she was laying on her back in what she figured was the middle of the bed, he pulled one of the earbuds out of her ear.

"What's your safe word, Remisha?" he asked her, as he ran his tongue behind her ear and kissed her softly on the neck just below it.

"Chocolate," Remisha said softly, her breathing was becoming heavy with anticipation. Even in all of her nervousness, she already was getting hot and bothered, she had no idea what Nieko was about to do to her but she wanted it, she wanted him any way she could have him.

"Noted. Now, a little more about this game we're about to play. It has two parts actually, I will get to learn more about you and your beautiful body, see what really turns you on and how much pleasure you can actually take. And you, my beautiful one, get to learn a little more about punishments and how creative I can be when I'm handing them out. So let's begin." His laugh was sinister against her ear before he pushed the ear bud back in.

He took one of her wrists and tied something soft to it, then he stretched her arm far from her body, when his movements near her hand stopped she tried to move her arm and was met with resistance, he repeated the process three more times until he had successfully tied her arms and legs to the bed.

Realizing she was spread eagle and tethered, blindfolded and couldn't hear a damn thing had her trying to sit up, she felt herself beginning to panic.

Nieko's hand pressed her gently back down on the bed before she felt his weight on top of her, his still clothed erection pushed against her wet and naked middle. He kissed her lips softly at first then he grabbed her by the back of her head and forced his tongue inside of her mouth kissing her aggressively.

Remisha's fear gradually melted away as her tongue began to dance with his. He bit her on her neck sharply and then he was gone again. Remisha's breath caught in her chest as she waited for his next move, not being able to see or hear what was going on was exhilarating and scary as hell at the same time.

After several panic filled moments he was back, she felt his lips on her ankle, his tongue slowly dragged up the inside of her leg. She moved from side to side on the bed as much as the restraints would allow, one second she wanted to get away from his chill inducing lips, the next she prayed she could have his soft, full lips on her body forever.

When she felt his warm breath disturbing her pubic hairs, even more chills broke out all over her body. Her senses were tingling, her pussy was dripping wet. He tugged at her hairs gently with his lips before his fingers spread her lower lips apart and his tongue swirled around her clit before he drove it deep into her ocean.

"Fuccckk!" she moaned, raising her hips off of the bed, sensations moving through her in waves as Nieko's tongue moved in and out of her moist center. She felt his hand press her back down on the bed, firmly holding her in place while his tongue dived deeper coaxing her pleasure to the surface. Not being able to move, see, or hear made everything he was doing to her more pronounced, she was in sensory overload.

Nieko sucked the sweet juices raining down from Remisha's quivering core, his tongue moved from side to side in the most intimate of kisses. She felt herself begin to twitch as an orgasm whispered down her spine and centered in the nerve endings of her middle. Her clit throbbed and pulsed painfully as she fought the beginning of her journey to completion.

"Nieko, please baby!" she moaned loudly, begging Nieko to stop and not to stop at the same time. She closed her eyes tight behind the blindfold, and thrashed her head from side to side, fighting to move her hips when Nieko pulled his tongue from her wet tunnel and swirled it around her clit before biting it gently.

"Oh my damn!" Remisha cried and began to jerk and

convulse like she had just been struck by lightning, as his hand still kept her pinned to the bed and he paid homage to her most sensitive spot.

He alternated between swirling his tongue, biting, sucking and blowing on her overly sensitive pearl, the sweet mixture of pleasure and pain sent Remisha into orbit. She felt one of the biggest orgasms of her life building, violently raking its claws up her legs and erupting out of her center as she soared higher and higher.

"Oh my fucking god! Oh my muthafucking god! Damn Nieko Damn Nieko Damn!" Remisha chanted as she came over and over again in earth shattering waves. Nieko fastened his mouth back onto her opening and sucked in her sweetness like he would die of thirst without it.

The tidal waves of her orgasm seemed to go on for hours, all the while Nieko kept sucking and licking her, sending her crashing into the shore of pleasure over and over again.

Remisha panted heavily trying to catch her breath, tears of completion rolled from her eyes from beneath the blindfold, wetting her hair and the pillow beneath her head as wave after wave still shook her from the inside out.

His mouth left her suddenly, she shivered from the absence of his body heat and the aftershocks of her orgasm and waited. For several minutes she wondered where he was, what he was doing, she even thought, for a fleeting fearful moment, he just left her blindfolded and tied to the bed. Her breathing was just about back to normal when she felt his weight on the bed again and he slowly entered her.

She threw her head back, moaning as his massive intrusion filled her to the hilt. His mouth came down on one of her nipples sucking hard before he tugged at it with his teeth, he moved to her other breast sending new signals to her throbbing center, it took about a minute for her to realize Nieko had yet to move or thrust inside of her.

"Nieko, please, don't do this to me!" she whined, catching on to this part of his game, he had given her pleasure, now he was about to give her pain. The pain of not fucking her!

Nieko lifted his head up from her breast smiling evilly even though she couldn't see him, she caught on almost immediately.

"Time to have some fun," he murmured with an ominous chuckle. He returned his attention to her breasts. Her skin was so soft and tasted sweet, he was beginning to think he would never get enough of tasting it.

He squeezed both of her breasts together and moved his mouth from one to the other sucking hard on her nipples. He felt her pussy getting wetter around him, her walls undulated up and down his erection causing him to pause for a second to get his body in check. Shit, she felt fucking amazing, but as much as he wanted to grab her by the hips and fuck her deep and hard, he had a point to prove first.

Remisha's ears were ringing, tears of frustration burned behind her closed eyelids while Nieko's mouth and dick aided her descent into sexual madness and there wasn't a damn thing she could do about it. Because of how he had her set up, all she could do was feel.

The way he was positioned on top of her had her hips pinned to the bed with his body weight so she couldn't move them, she made the muscles of her pussy contract and relax up and down his shaft in an attempt to coax him to move.

She only succeeded in him biting her on both of her

nipples, hard, before making his dick jump inside of her and sending shockwaves of need up her spine.

"Nieko, please stop, I can't take it, either fuck me or don't but you need to stop playing!" Remisha cried, trying to pull her wrists free.

She felt the vibrations of his laughter as he stopped sucking on her nipples and moved his head higher kissing her shoulder, collarbone, and neck as he slid his hands underneath her ass and moved in and out of her once and stopped.

"Nieko, what the fuck?" Remisha yelled, feeling like she was about to explode from the need for this man surging through her veins.

She felt him jump deep inside of her again, before feeling the vibration of his laughter. She wanted to kill him! What the hell was wrong with him? This shit was not okay!

He was lying on top of her and she could feel his chest vibrating and pausing rhythmically, she figured out he was talking to her knowing good and damn well she couldn't hear what he was saying!

He started kissing all over her body, her lips, her breasts, her neck then he would pause talking to her again. Remisha was almost in tears! What the fuck was he saying to her? Why was he still torturing her?

She was about to start screaming she hated him at the top of her lungs like a banshee when she remembered something he said in the beginning, the game had two parts.

They would both learn something, he would learn more about her and her body, and she would learn a little more about punishments and how creative he was with them. This all started because she was disrespectful about the car situation and when they were eating lunch.

Nieko gripped her ass again and moved in and out of her one time, making her head spin and a light bulb flicker on in her brain. She took a cleansing breath and tried to stop panting and fighting against the restraints.

"Nieko, baby, I'm sorry for being disrespectful when all you were trying to do is keep me safe," Remisha sobbed, feeling like she was about to spontaneously combust from all the sexual energy swirling around in her body.

A second later she felt the blindfold being ripped from her eyes and saw Nieko reaching up, pulling the headphones out of her ears.

"About Goddamn time! Fuck Remisha!" he snarled and grabbed her hips and began pumping in and out of her aggressively.

"Yes! Oh God yes!" she screamed happily as he delivered punishing strokes over and over again to her quaking middle.

An hour later, Nieko straddled her naked body untying her arms from the headboard, she now saw he had used black silk scarves to bind her.

Her entire body was sore, her eyelids were heavy from the multiple orgasms Nieko had brought her to. She was actually happy he was driving her to Letecia's because she could barely hold her fucking head up!

Nieko reached behind him and untied her legs too before moving off of her and pulling her into his arms, grabbing a bottle of water that was on his bedside table and taking a drink. "You good?" he asked her, passing the bottle to her. Remisha lifted her head enough to drink the entire bottle of water and dropped her head back onto his chest sleepily.

"Mmm hmm, I'm freaking fantastic," she purred before closing her eyes and drifting off to sleep.

Clinton stared up at the house with his blood boiling, he saw Remisha go inside and saw KooKoo or whatever the fuck his name was working on her car for a little bit before he went inside too, that was at least an hour and half ago.

Remisha was beginning to really piss him off, first she acted all brand-new yelling and screaming for him to leave her house the other day when he remembered, back in the day, she used to beg him with tears in her eyes to stay. She actually had the nerve to just stand there silent while KooKoo's big ass flexed on him!

Yeah, he could tell he was going to have to step up his game and pull out the heavy artillery. Remind her why they would always be bound, and why he was still in possession of her heart.

Chapter 5

"So tell me again why Nieko had to drive you down here?" Letecia asked Remisha curiously, munching on the homemade Chex Mix Remisha brought her.

Remisha lifted her head off of the pillow she was lying on at her end of Letecia's giant sectional scrolling through the Netflix menu looking for something for them to watch. Brent was out of town as usual. "Lettie, I already told you, he said something about my car making a whining noise and wanted to fix it for me," she explained again, covering a yawn, and dropping her head back down heavily onto the pillow.

Even after an almost two-hour nap Remisha was still exhausted. She felt like she had worked out for twelve hours straight, her lady bits were sore but still singing the praises of Nieko King.

"Oh, okay, because I was beginning to think it was because he put something serious on your ass!" Letecia giggled, popping a Cheerio in her mouth and looking at Remisha with an arched eyebrow.

"Yeah, well that too," Remisha admitted, not even bothering to lift her head this time and waited for Letecia's reaction.

She had no idea why she tried to act like nothing happened between her and Nieko knowing Letecia could probably see it written all over her face, she pulled the sleeves down over her wrists to make sure the small friction burns from her fighting to get her hands loose were covered.

"Oh hell nah, heffa! Get yo ass up!" Letecia shouted, quickly crawling over to Remisha's end of the sectional. "I want to hear everything!" Letecia demanded, snatching the pillow Remisha was lying on from under her head.

"Lettie, come on, damn! I'm tired! Give me back my pillow!" Remisha whined, she sat up and tried to grab her pillow back from Letecia.

Letecia kept the pillow from Remisha's reach. "Not hardly, Remy, spill it!" she demanded, setting the pillow further away from Remisha before folding her legs underneath her hip and resting her head on her hand, her elbow was propped on the couch, looking at Remisha expectantly.

"Ugh! You stay on my nerves!" Remisha groaned loudly, kicked off the lightweight blanket she had covering her legs and instantly regretted it, both her sore legs and little sister protested loudly. "Oww!" she whined, squeezing her legs closed tight and falling back over on her side.

"Damn, like that, Remy?" Letecia teased with a wicked grin and a wink in Remisha's direction.

Remisha sat back up a little more gingerly than before. "Lettie the man is a god with a demon's dick!" she declared, closing her eyes remembering her afternoon adventure with Nieko. "I have never experienced *anything* like this man in my life!"

"Way to go, Nieko! You know this is the first time in a long time your stank ass attitude didn't enter the room before you did," Letecia quipped going back to her Chex Mix. "I know this is all new, but I honestly believe Nieko is really good for you, Remy and not just because he got you over there all glowing and shit either!" Letecia said, smiling over at Remisha approvingly.

Remisha leaned back on the couch and turned towards Letecia. "You think so, huh? Why? What about him makes you feel that way?" she asked curiously.

Letecia stood up to shake the crumbs off her leggings and sat back down facing Remisha. "Just look at today for example, not one of the men you have dated in the past would have even noticed your car was making a noise, let alone volunteer to fix it and drive you down here, unless there was something in it for them. From day one, Nieko has been looking out for you and treating you like a queen. I like that."

Remisha sighed. "True, but I can't lie, Lettie, I'm scared as hell. Most of my relationships are amazing coming out of the gate. But when the fairy dust settles, and he stops being so polite, that's when his true colors show. And let me tell you, I'm tired of finding out the magic is nothing more than a man behind a curtain creating illusions," Remisha admitted seriously, wishing sometimes she didn't think so much and was just able to go with the flow and let whatever was going to happen, happen.

Letecia grabbed Remisha's hand shaking her head. "Honestly, Remy, I don't think it's going to be like that this time, just give him a real chance," Letecia reasoned with a soft smile. "You know what's crazy? Normally, it's you trying to convince me that these pretty little mistakes, like Clinton, are the next best thing since sliced bread. Even though you already know they ain't about shit but you think you can fix them or something. Now for the first time, in the history of time, I'm sitting here telling you the man you're interested in is a good man, a damn good man and you're already trying to talk your way away from him," Letecia stated, shaking her head again.

"I'm not trying to talk my way away from him, Lettie. But after everything I went through with, and because of Clinton, is it a bad thing for me to want to guard my heart this time? I'm too old to rebuild my life if things fall apart again," Remisha reasoned pulling her hair up into a messy bun.

Leticia sighed. "Real talk, Remy. But hurt gonna come if it's meant to come and there is nothing you can do about it besides control the way you react to it. You can't control what Nieko is going to do, just don't be so focused on guarding your heart that you block the good things that are happening too."

Remisha squeezed Letecia's hands and rolled her eyes heavenward. "I love you, Lettie and I so hate it when you're right, you make me sick!" she teased, snatching the Tupperware container of Chex Mix from her to take a handful.

"Yeah, I love you too and that's how you know I'm a real one, I'm your mirror girl. Sometimes you ain't going to like what's staring back at you but it's the truest reflection of yourself you're ever gonna see," Letecia said snatching her Chex Mix back.

"Lettie, sometimes you sound like a damn fortune cookie, I swear to God!" Remisha told her laughing, throwing her arms around Leticia in a hug. "But thank you for being the no nonsense reflection my ass needs sometimes."

"How are you feeling after our little game today?" Nieko asked her over the phone.

Remisha blushed at the memories of how they spent their afternoon. After she and Letecia fixed Chicken Caesar salad for dinner together, Letecia fell asleep in the first twenty minutes of the movie they were watching, so Remisha called Nieko to tell him goodnight.

"Mmm, still tingling all over. I'm tired, but it's a good tired.

What about you Mr. King?" she asked, stretching her arms over her head before lying back on her bed.

When Letecia and Brent moved to San Diego one of the first things they insisted on was Remisha had to come down to pick and decorate her own room. She made it a point to have her room there be the exact opposite of her room at her house. Her room at home was decorated in dark wood and dark colors like, black, plum and gray. Her room at Brent and Letecia's house was decorated in soft pastels and white, it was a reminder not to take herself so seriously when she was there, not that Brent and Lettie would allow her to anyway.

The automatic smile on her face refused to be contained, just hearing his voice had her feeling giddy.

"Honestly wishing I still had you here with me. I can smell your perfume on my pillows and it's making me miss you more, but other than that I'm fine. I ran to the auto parts store to grab that part for your car so I can put it on tomorrow," Nieko told her, she could tell by his voice he was smiling too.

Remisha's mind flashed back to what Letecia said earlier, how no other man she dated had ever bothered to do anything for her that wasn't self-serving. The one and only time Clinton even bothered to wash her car was after he borrowed her car to drive out of state. Freaking 'Fortune Cookie Lettie' strikes again!

"If I didn't say it earlier, I really appreciate you working on my car for me, I'll have to cook you a special dinner or something to pay you back." She smiled, playing with the few curls that escaped her bun, she pulled one straight to see how long it was and let it go then grabbed another one and did the same thing.

Her call waiting beeped, Remisha sat up to check her phone with a frown since it was getting a little late and saw that Nieko was calling her but it was a video call, she answered it with a curious frown.

"I needed to see your face when I said this," he said when her face popped up in the chat. His expression looked like something serious just happened, making her even more confused. "Remisha, I don't need to be rewarded for doing what a man is supposed to do for his woman. You, your happiness, and your wellbeing are a reflection of me and how well I treat you. You want to show your gratitude? Carry yourself like the cherished woman you are now, and I know you to be even when you're not with me, that's all I ask for." When he was finished, even over the video connection, she could see his dark eyes shining.

Remisha looked at him, nodding slowly. Fuck! He was so intense sometimes and she loved it! His demanding ways were hotwired to her hormones. Still, she didn't mean for her offer to cook him dinner to be taken that way. "Nieko, I'm sorry. I obviously offended you but it wasn't my intention at all. I was just saying I appreciate you even noticing something was going on with my car, let alone being willing to fix it," she explained, sitting up putting her back against the headboard.

"I'm not offended, beautiful. I just want you to know what kind of man you're dealing with, that's all. Now, if you want to cook me dinner because you want to spend time with me I'm all for that, lunch was good as hell earlier," he said with a smile creeping across his face.

Remisha smiled, shaking her head. One thing was for damn sure, she would never be bored dealing with Nieko's impassioned ass! "I'm glad you liked it, anytime you're ready the invitation is open, just let me know my kitchen or yours."

Nieko's smile turned wicked. "You tell me, especially considering what happened when you cooked in my kitchen." He caught his bottom lip between his teeth looking sexy as hell to Remisha.

"You know I meant to ask you about that, why did you make a big production grabbing all of that stuff out of the kitchen not to use any of it on me today?" she asked curiously, remembering him silently moving through the kitchen earlier.

"Oh, I had every intention of using them all but after tasting you, plans changed. I'm sure we will revisit them one day." He nodded thoughtfully, his eyes were getting low and sleepy.

Remisha felt her pussy twitch at the thought of another game and lesson. "Hmm, maybe but that's a conversation for another time. It's getting late and you look like you're running out of steam and rightfully so, you put in some serious work this afternoon." Her smile told him exactly where her mind was even if her mouth had not.

"As did you, beautiful one, you caught on to my game pretty fast, and leading up to the end of it? You tasted incredible," He told her using his hand to cover his yawn. "Well, enjoy your time with Letecia and I look forward to seeing you Sunday afternoon. Sleep well, Remisha and dream of me."

Remisha was still staring at her phone smiling like a fool at this handsome man who was slowly but surely sweeping her off of her feet. "I already do that while I'm awake," she admitted smiling even bigger. "Goodnight, Nieko and see you Sunday."

"Oh my goodness look at how cute these are!" Remisha rushed over and picked up three designer onesies that said 'Auntie's Little Diva' in different colors and held them up for Letecia to see the next day, Saturday afternoon.

"Remy, no! Don't you dare start shopping for these babies yet, we don't even know what the sex is," Letecia protested taking the shirts away from Remisha and dragging her away from the baby section all together.

"Ugh, you are no fun! How soon you forget how you were

with–" Remisha stopped walking as her breath caught in her chest, her bright smile fell.

Letecia immediately knew where Remisha's thoughts had taken her and grabbed her in a tight hug in the middle of the aisle in Macy's. "I remember. Remy. I remember everything I bought for her, I kept it all just like I promised," she assured Remisha before letting her go and wiping away a few tears. "Tell you what, I'll make you a deal, the minute we know the sex of the babies, you can go buck wild and I won't say a word, okay?" Letecia linked arms with Remisha smiling again and led her out of the store.

"All right Lettie, remember you said that when you have to buy a bigger house because all the stuff they have from Auntie Remy is taking over, you better not say a word!" Remisha warned, wiping away a wayward tear of her own.

"I won't, I promise! So Auntie Remy, I know we just had breakfast like an hour ago but can we grab a snack? I am starving!" Leticia said, moving in the direction of the food court.

"Girl, *you* can have a snack. I can't eat every time you get hungry, I'll be three-hundred damn pounds! Yeah, Brent needs to change his schedule already so he can be your food buddy, either that or he's paying for my lap band surgery when you have the babies!" Remisha said, as she pushed her dark and woeful thoughts to the back of her mind and smiled at Letecia. She refused to let her past tragedy ruin her sister/friend's excitement and happiness.

"As I said over the phone we would like to offer you a one-time contract to write a book. Your short stories are well received and extremely popular, we believe a book would be very successful and lucrative for us all," Yvette, Remisha's editor-in-chief from Essence, told her at lunch the following Monday.

Even though this opportunity was incredible news, Remisha had her reservations. She wasn't sure if she could commit let alone complete an entire book with everything else in her life that required her attention.

"I have to say thank you so much for your confidence in me and for this opportunity, Yvette, but I would like to take some time to review the contract and think about it. Would I be out of line to ask for a week or so to mull things over?" Remisha asked carefully, one of the reasons she never pursued a career as a novelist was because she liked the ebb and flow of writing when she felt like it and for the most part she would much rather leave the story telling to the authors she edited for.

"Of course, I don't see a problem with that at all. Just call my office to set up a meeting when you are ready to discuss the matter further," Yvette replied, pulling a folder out of her brief-case and placing it in front of Remy before gathering her things to leave and standing up.

Remisha stood too and shook Yvette's hand. "Sounds good and I promise I won't take too long to review everything and make a decision. I just need to make sure I have the time to dedicate to such a huge undertaking. Out of curiosity which one of my shorts prompted this idea?" Remisha asked, not wanting to assume which one it was.

Yvette flashed her a cynical smile. "'Chocolate' of course. You sent our readers into a frenzy with that one," she said holding her briefcase in front of her with both hands.

"Last question, would you expect the book to be based on that short story or would I be free to write something else?" Remisha asked, biting the inside of her cheek thoughtfully.

"You'd be free to choose but, I have to say, I believe a book based on 'Chocolate' would do quite well."

Remisha nodded thoughtfully. "I'll keep that in mind when making a decision and thank you again for allowing me some time." Remisha shook her hand again.

"No problem, Remisha, and I look forward to speaking with you soon," Yvette shook her hand and walked out of the restaurant, Remisha reclaimed her seat pulling out her phone.

"Hello beautiful, how did your meeting go?" Nieko asked her when he answered his phone.

She smiled instantly. Normally she would have called Letecia first with a dilemma but she already knew where she stood on this particular matter, Lettie had been telling her she needed to write a book for years. So right now she needed another opinion.

"It went well. I was wondering, do you have time for lunch? If not, I understand. We can talk about it later on," Remisha asked, thanking the waitress for a lunch menu and a refill on her green tea.

"Tell me where you are?" he requested, she could hear him typing.

"I'm at Rio City Cafe, is that too far? Like I said, if you don't have time we can meet up later," Remisha told him, drinking her tea.

"If you wanted to talk about it later, you wouldn't have called me now, Remisha. I'll be there in thirty minutes, sit tight and see you soon, beautiful," Nieko said before hanging up.

Remisha shook her head, smiling she as she put her phone back in her purse and started looking at the menu.

"Well, well, well, if it's not my number one girl," Clinton said as he dropped in the seat across from Remisha about ten minutes later. After deciding what she wanted to eat she was reading the contract from Yvette with a highlighter in her hand.

Remisha rolled her eyes and kept on reading the contract, the man was like a recurring yeast infection. "I'm not your anything, Clinton. So is it safe to say you're stalking me now?" she asked, still not looking at him.

Clinton's presence was a reminder of some of the darkest days of her adult life, and the fact he kept approaching her as if nothing happened made her want to do him bodily harm.

"Nah, it's never that serious. I just happened to be meeting someone for lunch and saw you sitting over here all by your lonesome and wanted to say hello and check on you as well," Clinton explained, leaning across the table casting a shadow on what she was reading.

Remisha re-capped her highlighter and pushed the contract back into the folder before folding her hands in front of her and glaring at Clinton. "I won't be alone for long, Nieko is on his way and even if he wasn't, me sitting alone is not an open invitation for you to sit down. Considering you are the only point of contention in my otherwise wonderful life, you didn't need to check on me. How many times and how many ways do I have to say I want nothing to do with you? Is English no longer your primary language or something?" she asked, her eyes narrowed and hostile.

Clinton rolled his eyes and sat back sucking his teeth, she could feel the jealous energy rolling off of him. "So that's your man now, huh? You and I both know he will never hold a permanent place in your heart like I do, so I ain't tripping." He smirked resting his elbows on the table with a smile.

Remisha stared at him dumbfounded. "Clinton, how is it that you are so full of yourself you can't even hear or comprehend when you are being rejected? You don't have a special place on the bottom of my shoes let alone my heart. Again, if this sudden and annoying reappearance in my life has anything to do with that short story, let me reiterate, it was just a story, a work of fiction. If anything it was my love letter to the man I have always dreamed about having in my life and you, Clinton are not nor were you ever him, so you need to stop breaking your arm patting yourself on the back like you were. You really want to touch my heart with a grand gesture? Stop the good guy act, forget you ever saw me again, and leave me alone," Remisha said, sounding a lot calmer than she actually felt.

"Whatever, Remy. Despite you treating me like a stepchild, I'm still checking on you because I heard through the grapevine your girl is pregnant and wanted to know how you were holding up." he said, staring at her and leaning forward. "Let me ask you this, do you ever think about her, Remisha? She would have been in school by now, right?" Clinton asked her with a serious expression. "Does 'Mr. Right Now' know anything about her? Or the reason she's not here? What about the fact I will be the only man who can ever say we went half on a baby?" he spat, his jaw worked slowly as his eyes narrowed at her with hostility.

"Finally. Welcome back to the Clinton I know! I was beginning to wonder where that selfish, bastard side went," Remisha said, sitting back in her chair crossing her legs. "First of all, I am over the moon excited for Letecia and Brent so miss me with your bullshit ass feigned concern. The fact you would even think I would have anything but happy feelings about Lettie being pregnant just goes to show how petty and small minded you still are. Secondly, you have no right to mention, let alone ask me, anything about her, ever!" Remisha hissed, feeling her face growing hot in anger, violent thoughts rolled around in her head about him and that vindictive, insecure bitch Melissa. "You can spin what happened any way that helps you sleep at night but we both know the truth and who is really at fault here. Now you need to get the fuck up right now and don't look back, of all the subjects you can bring up about our past, she is, and will always remain, untouchable," Remisha hissed through clenched teeth as she shook all over and blinked away tears.

"Yeah, okay. Typical Remisha, still blaming me. Acting like I didn't lose you both on the same day. No matter what you say, you know what you did and we will always be linked, our daughter makes it so." Clinton scoffed and pushed away from her table and sauntered away.

Nieko watched from the entrance as Clinton walked away from Remisha after what looked like a heated exchange. His patience with the man was wearing very thin. Nieko wasn't a jealous man, he had no reason to be, but the way Clinton kept circling around Remisha was starting to get on his damn nerves. He might have to step in and handle the situation if it continued to happen. No one messed with what was his.

"Hey beautiful, have you ordered yet?" Nieko asked, leaning down and kissing her softly when he reached her table. He took off his suit jacket and hung it on the back of his chair, his less than kind thoughts about Clinton forgotten the minute he saw Remisha's beautiful face light up when she saw him.

"Hey handsome, you got here sooner than I thought and no, I didn't order yet. I was waiting for you but I know what I want," Remisha answered with a bright smile, touching his face. He noticed her eyes were a little red, like she had been crying, he didn't like that shit one bit. Yeah, Clinton had one more time to step to her and it would be him he was dealing with, not Remisha.

"Okay, let me catch up and decide what I want to eat then. Can't have you in here starving," he said with a wink, sitting down and picking up the menu looking at her. "Are you good?"

he asked with a look of concern, he hoped she knew she could talk to him about anything.

Remisha sighed picking up her water glass. "Yeah, I'm fine. Clinton just left, I'm surprised you didn't see him. I guess he's meeting someone here for lunch and saw me and couldn't resist coming over to get on my damn nerves," she explained to Nieko, swirling the water around in her glass, her eyes shining a little from unshed tears.

"Hmm, looks like he succeeded. Anything you want to talk about?" Nieko offered, closing his menu and putting it on the table giving her his undivided attention. He didn't mention Clinton himself because he trusted Remisha and felt if she wanted him to know about their conversation she would tell him like she just did.

"No, not really, besides, I refuse to allow him to disrupt our time together, as a matter of fact we have spent too much time talking about him already, so next subject, please. What looks good to eat?" she asked resting her elbow on the table and looking at him, her eyes traveling from his clothes to his face.

―――――

"So what are your first thoughts on it? I know this is a huge opportunity but is it what you want to do? Is it the next step in your career path?" Nieko asked her after she told him about the offer from Yvette.

"Like I told Yvette, I really want to think about it and make sure it's what I want to do. I like the freedom editing and free-lance gives me," Remisha told Nieko, reaching over and eating a tortilla chip off his plate, her eyes traveling over him again, she loved how he looked in a suit and tie.

He gave her a withering look when she stole a second chip. "I get that, just don't talk yourself out of it because you're afraid to do it or something. You said the short story was successful, maybe the book will be, too. And for the record, woman I asked you did you want to share nachos, and you said 'no' because of all the junk you ate with Letecia this weekend, now you're sitting here stealing all mine," Nieko fussed with a frown. For some reason it made Remisha laugh.

"Aww poor baby, Nieko don't like sharing!" Remisha teased laughing even more, her conversation with Clinton moving further and further from the forefront of her mind.

Nieko's dark eyes flashed for a moment. "Keep it up and we are going to cut lunch short," he threatened, looking stern.

Remisha's eyes narrowed playfully, there was no way a few chips warranted discipline so she called his bluff and pulled another chip from his plate. "Well, if I'm already in trouble I might as well make it worthwhile. You might want to eat some before they're all gone, you know get your strength up." She shrugged and winked at Nieko enjoying her chip.

Nieko stared at her, still looking cross while wiping his hands on his napkin, nodding slowly. And for a split second, her smile slipped, thinking he was actually serious until she saw a tug of his sexy smile on his lips.

"Damn, you are so beautiful, Remisha, especially when you're like this, I like this side of you. The longer I know you the more I have come to realize I love everything about you." He reached across the table taking both of her hands in his. "I wish I didn't have a meeting in a few hours, I would love to make you laugh like this all afternoon," he told her, smiling even brighter.

Remisha reached up and caressed the side of his face, even though she loved his normally baby-smooth skin she liked how his stubble felt under her fingers. "Thank you, Nieko, I love everything about you, too, and you do know, my smiles and good vibes these days have a lot to do with you, right? Even Letecia keeps saying I'm not as evil lately," she admitted, blushing a little, loving the moment they were in, not wanting their impromptu lunch date to end.

Nieko reached out and took her hand from his face and kissed the palm of her hand. "That's good to know, Remisha because I feel the same way about you," He told her, smiling and kissed her hand again.

He happened to glance over her shoulder and saw Clinton watching them intently from the other side of the restaurant, his lunch date might as well be talking to herself for all the attention he was paying to her. When his and Clinton's eyes met, Clinton's curious stare became a hostile glare.

Remisha frowned in surprise as Nieko's sweet smile disappeared and was replaced with a serious glare over her shoulder. She turned her head and knew immediately it was Clinton that Nieko was glaring at because Clinton was also glaring at him.

"Shit," Remisha mumbled to herself, knowing how persistent and intent on proving a point Clinton could be, and how no nonsense Nieko was. She could tell these two men were going to clash at some point and it was going to get ugly.

Clinton was still heated and he wished this damn girl he invited to lunch would just shut the fuck up! His goal, when he invited her here, was for Remisha to see them together and get jealous, see what she was missing. Instead she was over there touching on Nemo, or whatever she said his name was, and shit, while he was stuck with 'Babbling Bonita' here!

He knew bringing up the daughter she lost was below the belt but he needed a direct hit, something to get her fucking attention! He was tired of her fucking games and attitude, yeah she lost a baby and couldn't have anymore but what about him? He lost the baby, too and even though he was relieved when it happened, he came to realize something that belonged to him was snatched away because of her carelessness. Yeah, he kept telling Melissa that Remisha was still chasing him but the accident was her own damn fault and here he was still willing to forgive her selfish ass!

Since she wanted to play rough, that was what they were going to do, and when he was finished, "Nemo" would be a fucking memory.

Chapter 6

"Lettie, I swear to God, Clinton is going to make me hurt his ignorant ass! He sent me another package and this was petty as fuck and completely uncalled for!" Remisha snapped two weeks later trying to control her emotions, staring down at the package from Clinton sitting on the couch next to her and resisted the urge to call and cuss his ass all the way out because she knew that was the reaction he wanted.

She had foolishly thought since she hadn't heard from, seen, or received anything from him in the last two weeks that he had finally got the message to leave her alone until the unmarked package arrived, it was sitting on her porch when she got home. It was a glass picture frame that said 'Family' on it with two photos in it, one of him and her on their last weekend together, the second was an ultrasound picture, the only picture she ever gave him of their daughter she lost because of him and his cheating ways.

"Girl, what did the bastard send this time? I promise you Clinton don't want me coming for his ass! You saved him from death once, it won't happen again," Letecia snapped loudly.

Remisha ran her hand down her face in frustration, immediately regretting her decision to call Letecia. The last thing she needed was Letecia getting upset because of this kind of unnecessary shit, but she couldn't call Nieko like she wanted to either because it looked like he was about five minutes off of Clinton's ass the last time they saw each other. Besides, they weren't at the point in their relationship where she wanted to bring all of this mess up anyway.

"Don't worry about it, Lettie. I'll handle it. Just calm down, the last thing I need is you getting all riled up over something stupid that Clinton did. I'm sorry I even called you with it. You just worry about taking care of yourself and those babies." Remisha sighed, dropping the frame back in the box along with the card that came with it and setting it all on the floor on the side of the couch.

"Remy, you know the only reason why he's digging his heels in like this is because of Nieko right? And I hate to be the one to say I told you so with that damn story, but I told you so! You are like the skeptical character in all the supernatural movies who fucks around and wakes up some angry ass evil spirit! Clinton is a narcissistic asshole who thinks he is the best thing that has happened to the world since Christ walked the earth. In his twisted way of thinking, there is no way you could ever be completely done with him ever, and because you two have a loss in common he thinks he's special, wears that shit like a badge of honor. I wouldn't be surprised if he used it to gain sympathy to get some," Letecia told her matter of factly sounding calmer much to Remisha's relief.

"Ugh, again with your fortune cookie ass, Lettie! I promise you that is pretty much what he said the last time I saw him!" Remisha laughed, shaking her head.

"Girl, it has nothing to do with that, it's because I know assholes and how they operate and Clinton is their lord and savior!" Letecia snapped, chewing on something. "Oh, and before I forget, I need more cookies when you come up this weekend. I swear Brent ate all of the other ones, I had like two of them!" she fussed while still chewing.

Remisha shook her head, laughing. "I got you, but I have to ask, if you're not eating butter cookies what are you eating so aggressively?" she asked standing up to go start dinner for her and Nieko.

"Chex Mix! I hid the entire container from your brother-in-law so I still have some! I didn't even know that men could get pregnancy cravings and you want to know what his ass is craving, every homemade thing you make me!" she said loudly around a mouthful of Chex Mix.

"And let me guess, you are craving cookies at the moment? You know if you can't wait four days until I get there I can send you the recipe or walk you through making them," Remisha suggested with a smile pulling out the mallet to tenderize the chicken cutlets she was making for dinner.

"Yes! Tomorrow, okay? I'll make him a batch and you can make mine when you get here. So what are you and Nieko up to tonight?" Letecia asked Remisha, sounding happier.

"Um, just dinner and a movie, can you believe he has agreed to watch *"Memoirs of a Geisha"* with me?" Remisha asked, putting Letecia on speakerphone.

"Uh duh, Remy! If you told the man you wanted to go see Disney on Ice, he would take you and even wear mouse ears that light up! You have him so sprung it's ridiculous." Letecia snorted, she wasn't eating anymore.

"Shit, he ain't the only one I promise you! Girl, do you have any idea how many times a day I check my phone to see if he messaged me? And when he does I get all giggly and giddy. At first, I didn't think it was possible, but I really like Nieko," Remisha confessed, running water in a pot to cook the bowtie pasta for their bowtie alfredo.

Letecia snorted again. "Tell me something I don't know,

Remy. I think it's safe to say your evil ass has fallen completely in love with Nieko King," she teased Remisha in a singsong voice.

"Whatever, it ain't that serious, Lettie, but I have to go. I need to finish cooking and get cleaned up before he gets here," Remisha said, picking her phone up off the counter to check the time. He would be there in an hour and a half.

"Says the woman who is most definitely not in love!" Letecia teased. "Have fun, Remy. Tell Nieko I said 'Hi' and that he needs to come up soon to meet Brent since it looks like he will be around for a while."

Remisha rolled her eyes at her phone, trying not to smile. "You talk a lot of shit for a woman in desperate need of butter cookies. Keep playing if you want to, Letecia," Remisha warned calmly.

"Remy! You better call me tomorrow and help me make these damn cookies!" Letecia shouted, her voice on speaker-phone echoed through Remisha's kitchen.

"Good night, Lettie and tell Brent I said, 'Hello and I'm sorry about his cookies'," Remisha sang as she hung up her phone with Letecia still loudly protesting and begging her to stop playing.

***

Remisha had just pulled her hair up into a high ponytail with bangs when her doorbell rang, she slipped on her house shoes and rushed to answer it. She threw open the door with a huge smile on her face which quickly fell when she saw the murderous look on Nieko's face.

"We need to talk," he said, as he crossed the threshold and walked into the living room after giving her a quick kiss on the cheek and handing her a dark purple orchid.

Since she had agreed to explore their relationship on his terms, he had switched from giving her lilies to giving her orchids, she had no idea why but she loved both types of flowers anyway and pressed them in a sketchbook.

Remisha followed him into the living room looking apprehensive and confused. "Okay, should I serve dinner while we talk or wait?" she asked quietly, wondering what in the hell was going on.

"I'd prefer to get this out of the way before we eat, I didn't want to spend any time talking about it but now it's a very necessary conversation," Nieko explained, following her to the kitchen while she turned down the burners on the stove and covered the garlic knots she made earlier with a towel to keep them soft.

When she was done, Nieko took her by the hand and led her to the couch and sat down, taking both of her hands in his, looking up at her. "Like I said under normal circumstances I wouldn't even bring this subject up but, because of something I received today, I believe it's unavoidable. Talk to me, beautiful, tell me all about Clinton Maxwell and Sarai," he requested, looking up at her and still looking like he was about to kill somebody, at least now she knew who it was and now he wasn't the only one contemplating murder one.

Remisha's body jerked in reaction, she took a deep breath and sat down next to Nieko, "Can I ask what he sent you first?" she asked nervously, shaking all over.

Nieko kissed both her hands before pulling something out of his inside jacket pocket and putting it on the coffee table. It was a small frame with a copy of Sarai's ultrasound and a small card that read: *She's not the woman you think she is, ask her about Sarai.*

Remisha felt her blood boiling as she looked from the frame to Nieko, Clinton had gone too fucking far! Her chest felt tight as anger rolled through her body and caused her to shake all over. He had no right to bring her up at all, let alone bring her up to Nieko and he damn sure had no right to blame her for what happened! She suddenly heard the sound of hiccupped sobs and realized, to her dismay, it was her.

Nieko let go of her hands and went to the kitchen. He came back with a bottle of water and a cool towel. He pulled her into his arms and pressed the towel to the back of her neck as she sobbed. She hated Clinton, hated him for what happened and hated him for what he was trying to do to her and Nieko.

Nieko patiently waited for Remisha to cry it out and calm down. Since the package came all he wanted to do was find Clinton and break his fucking neck. This was a low blow and to bring up something that was obviously very painful to someone he probably claimed to love at some point, if not still loved now was some punk shit.

When her shoulders were no longer shaking from sobbing, he helped her sit up and gave her the bottle of water to drink. When she drank over half of it, he sat back gathering her in his arms and kissing her on the forehead.

"Better?" he asked, using his finger to tilt her head up so she was looking at him.

Remisha nodded and took another deep breath. "Yeah, I'm sorry, it's just I haven't heard anyone say her name in over five years. I sincerely hate, in a moment of weakness, I told him what her name was," she explained, fighting back more tears.

"I'm sorry, I didn't know what to expect but I would have never said it had I known this was how you would react to it. We don't have to talk about this if it's too painful, Remisha," he told her softly, leaning forward and pressing his lips to hers.

"No, it's okay, not talking about it will make Clinton think he has the upper hand or some shit," Remisha said, taking the towel from the back of her neck and using it to clean her face.

"Whenever you're ready, beautiful." He sighed and pulled her even closer.

Nieko felt her snuggle as close as she could to him and she brought her legs up on the couch, he rubbed her back to help her relax a little more. She was still and quiet for the longest time, he was about to ask her if she was okay when she started to speak.

"Remember on our first date and I told you how that Melissa chick cost me over $8000 when she egged and keyed my car? Well, that wasn't the only thing she damaged, she pushed me down a flight of concrete stairs because she got it in her head I was faking being pregnant to keep Clinton around," Remisha said in a rush, her voice was shaking with emotion.

"Melissa wasn't just a woman scorned, she was a woman obsessed and she was, and obviously still is, obsessed with Clinton. About three months after that Sunday when we found out about each other, I found out I was pregnant. I decided I was going to keep the baby, so I told Clinton. He threw an absolute fit at first, saying he wasn't ready to be a father, accused me of trying to trap him even though I was the one who ended our relationship the night I found out about Melissa, but my favorite lie was, of course, the baby wasn't his. I told him that was fine. I only told him because morally he had a right to know. But I didn't want, or expect anything from him, especially for us to be together. I would raise my baby on my own, my telling him was just a courtesy, that's it. Well for some reason, my indifference and not wanting to be with him, especially while I was pregnant with his baby, flipped a switch or something in him because suddenly I was getting daily texts checking on me, asking me did I need anything, and eventually he begged for one of my ultrasound pictures that he hung on his refrigerator. The only reason why I know where he kept it is because he sent me a picture of it hanging there. So did Melissa when she started harassing me by telling me she got my baby's daddy on lock, shit like that. The funny thing was I didn't care! I was done with Clinton and didn't want anything from him." Remisha paused and sat up to finish the rest of her water.

Nieko got up and grabbed them both another bottle of water after he turned the burners off on the stove. He had to do something with the angry energy he felt at the moment. This Clinton dude was complete trash as far as he was concerned, he idly wondered how Remisha was ever even with someone like that. More than that, how the fuck does he still fuck around with the crazy ass female that killed his daughter and basically tried to kill his baby's mom?

He came back to the living room and reclaimed his spot on the couch and pulled Remisha back into his arms. "Still good?" he asked, resting his chin on top of her head.

"I'm good," she answered and took the water bottle he offered her. "Anyway, the whole time he's trying to weasel his way back into my good graces and my bed, he's telling Melissa I'm chasing him and demanding we be together for the baby. At least that's what I assumed he was doing because of the way she was coming at me about him. Somehow she got my phone number and called and texted me relentlessly, telling me I could never have him, she was never going to let him go and finally that she believed I was faking being pregnant and the ultrasound picture I mailed him was something I downloaded off of the internet and she was going to expose me. I mean she was really losing her shit over this," Remisha paused and took a few deep breaths. Nieko, who normally didn't have a violent bone in his body, was so heated by her story so far, he was close to telling her to stop and going out to find the fool!

"The day of my baby shower, all hell broke loose. Letecia went all out and planned a teatime baby shower for her princess, that's what she called Sarai. All my friends and cousins and co-workers were there, we were having a great time and then Melissa showed up drunk as hell. She yelled and screamed at me, started trying to push me down, and announced to everyone I was faking being pregnant to keep Clinton and I was conning them all.

"Nieko, let me tell you, I have never seen Letecia so mad in my life, she flew across that room and she tried to kill that damn girl. Security was called and the party was cut short. Letecia arranged for the party planner to clean up and have everything shipped to her house so we could get the thank you cards done at another time. She told me I was going to spend the night at her house to be on the safe side and she was having Brent come pick up my car. So I was waiting for Letecia to pull the car around on parking level four when it happened.

"Letecia had parked up on eight but I had to go to the bathroom half way up, so I got off the parking garage elevator to go to the restroom. I was taking the stairs back to the parking elevators when Melissa popped up out of nowhere and pushed me down the stairs. The last thing I remember was her standing over me, calling me a bitch before she kicked me in the stomach. I woke up in the hospital three days later with a concussion, no longer pregnant and recovering from a total hysterectomy. I never really paid attention to anything else after the doctor told me Sarai was gone so I honestly missed the entire reason for the hysterectomy, all I know is something ruptured when she kicked me."

Nieko sat there quietly and held Remisha while she silently cried, he could tell she was crying again because her tears were soaking through the front of his shirt. His mind was going a mile a minute, no wonder she was so standoffish when they met and so overprotective of Letecia. He had overheard several of their conversations with Remisha making sure Letecia was resting and eating well, she called or texted Letecia many times a day and never allowed her calls to go to voicemail.

"That is so fucked up, I'm so sorry you had to go through something like that, I really am. I'm still confused as to why Clinton is obviously blaming you and using the loss of your daughter to try to come between us, though," Nieko said, moving her bangs and kissing her on the forehead.

Remisha sat up and used the towel to wipe her face again. "Well, that's because of Letecia. According to her she came looking for me when I wasn't where I said I would be and she ran into Melissa, saw me at the bottom of the stairs, put two and two together and called 911 before proceeding to beat the dog shit out of Melissa. The story Melissa told Clinton was that she was trying to leave and got turned around because she was tipsy, we saw her, jumped her, and she pushed me to get me off of her and that's how I fell. Why he decided to believe her and not me? I have no fucking idea. I didn't care then nor do I care now. The bottom line is my daughter is dead because he continued to play with the mind and the heart of a very unstable woman by lying about me to stroke his bruised ego when I rejected him." Remisha opened the second bottle of water and drank it all.

"Was Melissa charged with anything?" Nieko asked, still lightly rubbing her back, the more she said the more violent his thoughts got, he was willing to bet the day he met her for lunch and saw Clinton leaving the table he was messing with her about it then, too.

Remisha chuckled and scoffed. "That is the most unfortunate part of it all. There were no cameras in the stairwells so it was my word against hers and considering she was pretty messed up because of Letecia, they refused to file any charges against her for assault on me, they called it mutual combat so she got away with it. So yeah, now you know my saddest truth of all. I tried to be a good person and let him know I was pregnant. That was it and because of his fixation on me and her obsession with him, my daughter died and I can never have children."

Nieko gathered her in his arms again as she dissolved into another fit of tears. The thought of someone being so hateful to Remisha was a lot to wrap his head around and had him seeing red. Clinton Maxwell was a sick bastard who was using an unfortunate connection between them to keep messing with her peace of mind but that shit was coming to an end.

"Shh, I know it hurts, beautiful but I promise you this, you will never be hurt like that again, by him or anyone else. You're my lady and I love you, Remisha, and I will do whatever it takes to make and keep you happy, always."

Remisha sat up and looked at Nieko blinking away her tears, he was watching her intently, his eyes sparkling with emotion. "Nieko, did you just say you love me?" Remisha asked, her heart's rhythm picked up, pounding hard in her chest.

Nieko's face spread into his sexy smile and he chuckled. "Yes, Remisha, I just said I love you, why are you surprised? You had to know I had some deep ass feelings for you, woman," he stated, reaching out and touching her face.

After all she had been through and everything she just shared with him, nothing gave her greater joy or tremendous fear at the same time. She had reminded herself over and over again that Nieko was nothing like Clinton and let her guard down, but now here she was in uncharted territory and she didn't know how to feel. True, he was saying the words she fought so hard not to say herself and those words gave her the courage to move one step closer to her happiness but she was still very afraid of the outcome.

She ignored the voice of anxiety beginning to bombard her with questions and let the words finally fall from her mouth, "I love you too, Nieko. I think I have loved you since the day we argued about you coming to pick me up or sending a car service. No man has ever gone that far to ensure my safety or dug their heels in to call me on my attitude the way you did and do. Every day I'm near you, is a day I fall deeper and deeper in love with you," she admitted, smiling at him with more tears forming in her eyes.

"Now those are the kind of tears I can get with," he whispered and pulled her close, kissing her deeply. "You are the most incredible woman I have ever met."

Her need for Nieko came out of nowhere as her tongue danced with his, she repositioned herself until she was straddling his lap. She kissed him all over his face before kissing him on his neck and moving her hands under his shirt to touch his muscular chest and arms. She felt him growing hard beneath her so she grinded on his growing erection.

Nieko pulled her head back by her ponytail and fastened his lips to the side of her neck, causing her to shiver. His lips traveled down to her shoulder as he reached down and pulled her shirt over her head, moved her bra and began to suck on her breasts. "You are so fucking sexy, Remisha," he whispered softly.

Remisha arched her back and held his head in place as he pulled and tugged on one of her erect nipples with his warm lips. Being Nieko's object of desire was becoming her newest happy place.

His hands trailed down her sides to the hem of her jean skirt which he pulled up over her ample hips and ass, still driving her over the edge paying homage to her breasts. She felt him push her thong to the side and slide a finger inside of her, she came up on her knees to give him better access to her warm, welcoming center.

Nieko pulled his mouth away from her breast and pulled her ponytail again causing her to arch her back even more as his mouth traveled even further south, kissing and teasing her navel with his tongue. He moved his mouth back up her body, his soft lips skating all over her exposed skin, causing waves of frenzied heat to move throughout her body.

"You have my entire heart, beautiful," he whispered, unzipping his pants, freeing his erection. "If I have my way, you will never shed another tear of sadness again, only tears of joy. I promise you," he said emotionally, pulling her close.

"Damn, I fucking love you," Remisha moaned with her eyes closed. Tears spilled down her cheeks as he settled her over his erection and pulled her close as she began to ride him to her completion.

"So let me get this straight, this is supposed to be a romance?" Nieko asked Remisha with a frown taking a huge bite of his chicken and pasta. They were sitting on the floor in the living room eating dinner and watching *"Memoirs of a Geisha"*.

Nieko had pulled his pants back on sans underwear, he was shirtless and looking incredibly sexy to Remisha, even after their sexcapades on her couch and in the shower, her body was humming and ready for more.

Remisha shrugged looking over at him quickly before looking back at the TV, it was one of her favorite parts, the main character was going through her training in a montage.

"Yes it is, why?" she asked, finally dragging her eyes away and giving him her full attention.

"Her mother dies so her father sells her and her sister, then they get separated, she falls off of a roof and is told she is pretty much a slave for these people and now she is pining for a man old enough to be her damn daddy. Not to mention the abuse and beatings I've seen so far and she can't even be cool with her little homegirl anymore. Baby, what the hell is this?" Nieko complained standing up to take his plate back to the kitchen.

"It's a beautiful movie, just give it a chance." Remisha hit pause on the remote and followed him to the kitchen. "The costumes, the locations, and the women are all so beautiful," she reasoned, grabbing his plate and rinsing it along with hers and loading them in the dishwasher.

"So, in other words, we are watching a beautiful nightmare," he quipped, leaning on the counter and pulling her to him by the hips while she dried her hands on a kitchen towel.

When she was closer he leaned forward and kissed her softly on her neck. "Thanks for dinner, beautiful. Now I'm thinking I'm in need of dessert," he whispered, lightly biting her earlobe.

Remisha moved her head away from his wonderful lips. "What about the movie?" she asked, narrowing her eyes at him but still putting her arms around his neck.

"They already get their happily ever after, it's in the script. Now I'm trying to get mine." Nieko bent down, picked Remisha up, and sat her on the counter, his lips returning to her neck as he helped her out of her shirt.

Remisha closed her eyes and moaned when his hands came in contact with her sensitive nipples. "Mmm, good point."

"Nieko, why are we here?" Remisha asked, looking from him to the police station a few days later. Since she told him about Clinton and Sarai, he hadn't really let her out of his sight and now he brought her here, something else must have happened.

"We are here to file harassment complaints on Clinton. I went to go check my mail while you were in the shower and found these." He pulled three different style baby announcements cards out of his glove box, all of them had a copy of Sarai's ultrasound and the scribbled message, *'You will never have what we have, her heart belongs to me'*.

Remisha looked from the baby announcements to Nieko. "I don't understand, how the hell does he know where you live?" she asked, trying to wrap her head around what she was seeing.

"The only thing I can think of is he must have followed you to my house at some point. I think your boy is losing his damn mind and before I end up putting hands on him, we need to do this. You might even need to file a restraining order or something."

Remisha closed her eyes and covered her face and screamed into her hands. "God, how could I be so stupid? Lettie warned me this would happen but I didn't listen!"

Nieko moved her hands from her face and made her look at him. "What are you talking about, beautiful?" he asked her curiously with knitted eyebrows.

"Remember when I told you about my hesitations of writing a book based off of my short story *'Chocolate'*? Well, Lettie warned me that that short story would be like waking a sleeping giant and she was right, it brought Clinton back to California and back into my life. She told me he would think I was talking about him and come running," she admitted, so angry at herself for being so stupid!

She was rid of him, for five years, she had had no contact with the idiot and now because she wanted to prove she was finally over her hurtful past and could write a love story, he was back and not only harassing her again but now he was harassing Nieko too! She was surprised Nieko hadn't cut his losses and run for the hills. Who wants a woman with a crazy ass ex?

"Was *'Chocolate'* about him? Even loosely based on him at all?" Nieko asked her seriously.

"No, Nieko, not in the least. Hell, it's more about you than anybody else if you ask me, I just didn't know you yet," she admitted, sitting back and covering her face with her hands again.

He grabbed both of her hands again and held them tight. "Then stop blaming yourself for his bullshit," he demanded sternly. "If you have done nothing to encourage this man in any way, shape, or form then this is all on him, not you." His demeanor softened a little as he looked at her. "Now, that being said, you have to know and understand engaging him in conversation of any kind, knowing how messed up in the head he is, is encouraging him and I won't be pissed at him, I'll be pissed at you for putting yourself in harm's way again, understand?" he asked her, bringing her hands to his lips.

"I understand, and believe me I don't have a damn thing to say to the man," Remisha told Nieko, grabbing her purse to go inside the police station.

Letecia sat at her kitchen island with her mouth hanging open in disbelief when Remisha recounted the messed-up shit Clinton pulled by sending Nieko the framed picture of Sarai and her the pictures in the 'family' frame. "Remy, I simply cannot deal with that asshole! Who the fuck uses losing a child as a weapon to try to break up somebody's relationship?" she asked angrily, her face was bunched in a disgusted frown.

"Clinton Maxwell does, that's who but his little plan backfired because instead of pulling us apart, it actually brought us even closer together, but I still gotta wonder what his endgame is, you know? I mean even if me and Nieko broke up tomorrow, I would rather eat soup with a fucking fork with a gun to my head until I finish it, than deal with Clinton's stupid ass and he knows this!"

Remisha put two batches of butter cookies in the oven and joined Letecia at the kitchen island. "Wow, just wow. I can't say anything else about that headcase. What did Nieko say about everything?" Letecia asked, running her hand down her small round baby bump.

"Well, understandably so, he was pissed and after I told him the whole sordid story he just held me and told me he was sorry he had to even bring it up and that he loved me," Remisha told Letecia, casually picking up her phone to check her messages.

Letecia gasped and smacked Remisha's phone out of her hand. "Hold the hell up, Nieko dropped the 'L' word and you didn't call me as soon as he left? What the hell, Remy?" Letecia fussed, even though she was smiling and dancing excitedly in her chair.

"Well, because he didn't leave until this morning." Remisha smiled at Letecia and then even brighter when she heard her phone vibrate and saw she had a new message from Nieko.

"I talked to you Tuesday, Remisha, you mean to tell me you spent the last three days rolling around in bed with that man?" Letecia teased with a wicked grin.

"No, of course not! We had to take breaks and eat from time to time." Remisha laughed at Letecia's shocked expression. "No, seriously, we both just worked remotely from my place. I honestly think it was because he wanted to make sure I was okay after all of the stuff we talked about with the pictures and to be there just in case Clinton did another popup." Remisha smiled again, standing up to go check on the cookies.

"Aww! I love how protective of you he is. So tell me, Remy, when he said he loved you, did you say it back or did you leave the brother out there hanging with your evil ass?" Letecia asked, her eyes narrowing accusingly at Remisha.

"Whatever, Lettie, I'm not that evil and for your information, I told him I loved him too, not just because he said it either. I really do love him, I love him so much it's crazy. When I'm not with him all I want to do is call him so I can be with him again, the only time I don't feel that way is when I'm down here with you guys. Who would have ever thought I would be like this? Especially after all I've been through. I feel like I should be carrying around a notebook with our initials on it or something. I was so afraid of getting hurt again, Lettie but it's different with Nieko. I know in my heart of hearts he would never do anything to hurt me on purpose and let me tell you, it is an amazing feeling." Remisha moved the cookies from the cookie sheet to the cooling tray and came back to her phone.

His text, *Missing you, beautiful*, made her sigh instantly and smile even brighter at Letecia.

"Look at my girl finally getting hers! I love it! I'm so happy for you, Sis!" Letecia came around the island with tears in her eyes and hugged Remisha tight. "Now he for sure needs to come up here the next time you come when Brent is home."

Brent's ears must have been burning because he walked into the kitchen a few minutes later. He put four cookies on a saucer and another one in his mouth. Letecia glared at him when he leaned down and kissed her on the lips and touched her baby bump after he poured himself a glass of milk and walked back towards the den. "Perfect timing, Sis, it's halftime, take care of your sister and my babies while I finish watching the game please," Brent told Remisha around the cookie he still had hanging out of his mouth.

"I'm not playing, Remy, he is not going to make it through the rest of this pregnancy alive if he keeps eating all of my damn cookies!" Letecia threatened loudly over her shoulder in the direction of the den.

"Well, hell." Remisha sighed. She grabbed a glass bowl, set it in the sink under running hot water, while she took another two sticks of butter from the fridge and put them on a plate and put the warmed-up bowl over the plate to soften the butter. "Maybe we should postpone Nieko meeting Brent, at least until you start craving something he doesn't really like. I want Nieko to get to know my loving best friends, not *"The War of the Roses"* over butter cookies friends."

Chapter 7

Four months later

The more time that passed, the closer Nieko and Remisha became. They spent equal time at both of their houses but Remisha had to admit she loved her weekends at Nieko's best. Sometimes she would purposely step out of line just to be disciplined, even though he usually figured out what she was doing and she would get 'extra' from him, and corner time which she hated, for trying to manipulate the situation. But he and his creative punishments kept her senses soaring.

He had even started to accompany her down to Letecia and Brent's sometimes. Since the two men met they had really clicked and started hanging out, they usually spent their Saturdays watching sports or they worked on getting the nursery together.

Letecia and Remisha usually shopped or organized the obscene amount of baby things Remisha continued to buy for her two nieces and one nephew.

Remisha knew the time for her to relocate to San Diego

temporarily was approaching as Letecia's due date was drawing near and, while she was so excited to meet the babies, she was going to miss seeing Nieko daily.

Clinton seemed to have taken the hint and disappeared back under his rock and Remisha couldn't be happier about it, having her peace of mind back and the man of her dreams too. She had decided to take the book deal and after negotiating a very realistic deadline she was actually excited to write her first book. She decided to call it *'Sweet Cravings'* instead of *'Chocolate'*.

All in all, life was good and Remisha knew it would only continue to get better when the babies came.

"No, I can't leave work today. I'm sorry but I have played hooky and worked from home to be with you so many times in the past six months, Nieko, people at the office are forgetting what I look like," Remisha told him over the phone. He was trying to talk her into going to lunch and 'getting lost in the city' as he called it when they walked around all afternoon talking before going back either to her place or his place and getting lost in each other. She was in a perpetual state of bliss these days.

"Fine, Miss Editor, I guess we can just skip the lost in the city part and just meet up at my place then," he told her in a low and sexy voice.

Remisha crossed her legs when her middle began to thump and pulse at the thoughts that started running through her head. "Oh, no, Mr. Gamemaster, tonight is dinner at my place followed by the movie we still haven't finished watching because of your dessert loving ass and maybe some heavy petting and that's it," she countered with a face breaking smile. Remisha was determined they were going to finish watching *"Memoirs of a Geisha"* together if it killed her.

Every minute she spent with Nieko was never the same, just when she thought she knew what he was about to do next he changed up on her, she was never bored, the one and only predictable thing he did was distract her when it came to watching that movie.

"Baby, come on! That movie is so damn depressing, pick another one, any one and I promise you I will watch the whole damn thing, I will even bring popcorn," he said with a pitiful moan.

Remisha smiled a devious smile. "Okay, fine, but remember you said you will watch any other movie. So *"Sayonara"* it is. I'm leaving work at four today, so we can eat and watch the movie before you start your antics," she said knowingly.

"I could always just meet you at four, immediately start my antics and order takeout after we're done and then watch the movie," Nieko suggested with a seductive chuckle.

Remisha rolled her eyes laughing. "Whatever, man, just know we are finishing this movie tonight, Nieko," She said unable to stop smiling.

"Fine, Remisha, see your sexy ass in a few hours," he replied, still chuckling as he hung up.

"So, did you talk to Brent about what you two are going to do while we are having the baby shower at the house? I mean it's the only logical place that makes sense, especially with everyone buying three of everything, otherwise we are going to have to rent a U-Haul to get it all back to the house," Remisha asked Nieko going over her checklist for the shower again on the way up to Letecia and Brent's that Friday.

Nieko frowned looking her up and down before turning his

focus back on the road in front of him. "Yeah, we talked about it and we decided we are both staying in the house where all the party food is," he announced, looking rebellious.

"Nieko! You had one job! One and you couldn't even do that?" Remisha said looking at Nieko shaking her head disappointedly.

"Well, he made some good points. Yeah, we could go to a sports bar or something and watch football all afternoon with strangers eating mediocre bar food or we can stay in his den, watch football all afternoon and eat bomb ass food cooked by my beloved and beautiful girlfriend. I chose the latter, immediately," Nieko reasoned with maddening logic and a shrug.

"Wow, and did you two geniuses decide who was going to tell Lettie you two will be crashing her baby shower for the primary reason of eating the food?" Remisha asked, laughing as Nieko shot her a panicked look.

"I'm all about keeping my own woman happy, so that conversation is all on your Bro Bro," he said shaking his head in the negative. "Letecia is an absolute sweetheart until you get in the way of her and her cravings, and she has had Brent in her crosshairs for months now about that very subject, so yeah, I'm laying real low until she knows. I ain't crazy," Nieko said, grabbing her hand and bringing it to his lips.

Nieko told her only part of the reason he was more than happy to stay for the baby shower. He knew Remisha was genuinely happy for Letecia and Brent but just in case the shower brought back bad memories for her he wanted to be nearby.

"Ha ha, Nieko is afraid of a little bitty pregnant woman," Remisha teased and stuck her tongue out at Nieko. "Who would have thought my big strong man is a chicken?" she mused, shaking her head sadly.

Nieko suddenly veered right and took the next exit to get off the highway. Remisha frowned trying to figure out where they were going, he drove until he found a secluded area surrounded by trees and put the car in park.

Remisha looked around outside of the car to figure out what he was up to. "Nieko, where the hell are we? We gott–" Nieko cut her off by grabbing her by her chin.

"Stick your tongue out at me again and repeat what you called me," he demanded, his eyes flashing angrily.

Remisha's stomach dropped into her lap, she had gone too far with teasing him and hadn't even done it on purpose this time, oh shit! His grip on her chin tightened.

"Remisha, you know I hate to repeat myself, now stick out your tongue and repeat what you said," he growled, his deep, aggressive voice was basically hot-wired to her vagina, which started to twitch in anticipation immediately.

She took a deep, nervous breath, and licked her lips. "I said you were afraid of a little bitty pregnant woman and I called you my man and said you were a chicken," Remisha repeated, her voice soft and nervous before she stuck her tongue out at him again.

She had no idea what to expect next, especially since they were not at his house with his usual go to toys and she had to admit she was a little scared to find out what he was about to do to her.

"Interesting, so you think your man is a chicken, huh?" he asked, pulling her face closer to his over the car console. "And to add to the disrespect you stuck your tongue out at me?" Nieko tsked, lowering his lips to hers and kissing her aggressively, before letting her chin go. "And speak up, didn't I tell you when you do something I'm not happy with to own that shit?" he asked thoughtfully, still looking annoyed.

He took off his seatbelt and opened the door to leave the

car. "Let's go have a talk about your behavior," he said, smiling at her with an evil grin.

Remisha watched him leave the car and walk down a little way away from the car, deeper into the trees and lean on one of the trees staring back at her. She had yet to even take off her seatbelt, let alone open the car door and consider going over to where Nieko and his twisted thoughts were.

She jumped in surprise when her phone vibrated in her hand. "I would strongly suggest you join me now. If I have to come back up to get you, it won't be pretty," he said evenly when she answered, then hung up.

Remisha whimpered apprehensively as she unlocked her seatbelt, got out of the car and slowly made her way to where Nieko was leaning on the tree, he had one foot resting on the trunk, his muscular arms were folded, muscles bulging in his t-shirt as she moved closer.

"Have you ever heard of the phrase, 'Tree Hugger'?" he asked her with the same evil grin he had at the car.

Remisha nodded slowly, her heart was up in her throat. What the hell was he up to?

"Well, today, you get to be one. Here's the deal, you are going to hug this tree and no matter what you're not going to let go, every time you do I'm lighting that sexy ass of yours up, understand?" he asked, taking her by the hand and leading her closer to the tree he was leaning on.

What in the entire fuck? How the hell did he think of a punishment that damn quick? Remisha looked at him with a pleading look, he could not be serious! She whimpered again and regretted her decision to wear a maxi sundress for the drive down to San Diego as he positioned her the way he wanted her.

They were far enough off the road no one would see them if they drove by, but she was still wondering what in the hell he could possibly do to her that would make her let go of the tree.

Nieko lifted her dress over her hips and took off her thong. Before she could even have another thought he rammed himself deep inside of her.

"Nieko, goddamn!" she screeched as he began to pound balls deep inside of her, and she hugged the tree as tight as she could.

He grabbed her by the hips and pulled her into every one of his aggressive thrusts, her pussy burned and pulsed around his erection and his punishment continued. The louder she cried out the deeper and harder his thrusts went inside of her.

"That's right, yeah, own that shit!" he ground out through clenched teeth as he hammered deep inside of Remisha's wet opening.

Remisha felt her legs begin to shake, her arms slipped as she began to sweat, the minute one of her arms lost contact with the tree, Nieko's stinging smacks rained down her ass sending her senses reeling.

"Dammit, Nieko!" she cried out feeling like she was in heaven and hell at the same time as his assault on her wet pussy continued.

"Hug the tree, Remisha," He said repositioning his feet, grabbing her hips even tighter and switching up the angle of his thrusts. Every inch of his swollen erection was hitting her wet opening hard and deep, driving her insane.

"Fuuucckk!" Remisha hissed, coming up on her tiptoes in her sandals, as he forced himself even deeper inside her, her entire pussy pulsed and contracted around his violent intrusion.

With his strong grip on her hips and her hugging the tree she had no place to go, all she could do was absorb the strength of his thrusts while he powered on.

Her arms began to ache, her legs were buckling as she struggled to stay standing up. Nieko treated her ass to another series of smacks, picked up the pace and jackhammered in and out of her in rapid speed. She felt the veins of his dick pulse against her vaginal walls and the head of his dick swell as he drove himself as deep as he could and exploded inside of her.

"Oh fuck! Oh fuck! *Oh fuck!*" Nieko bellowed as he came, still moving in and out of her with determined purpose. Finally his hips slowed to a stop and he pulled himself from her soaked middle.

Remisha's panting breaths were making her dizzy, sweat dripped from her body as her pussy protested Nieko's absence. She was close to frustrated tears when she realized the real punishment was that she had not been allowed to come.

Nieko helped her stand upright again and pushed her up against the tree, kissing her aggressively before catching her bottom lip between his teeth. "That smart mouth of yours gets you every time, huh, Remisha?" he quipped with a wink and helped her back to the car.

Remisha gingerly got back into the car, her arms and legs were sore, her pussy was still pulsing with need, and for the first time since she met Nieko, she wanted to hurt his ass!

"Relax, beautiful, you have all weekend to earn all you're craving right now and more." He touched the side of her face, winking and smiling evilly again before pulling back onto the main road and eventually the highway.

Yeah, she was gonna kill him!

"I can't believe how much stuff they got for the babies, scratch that, how much *you* bought for the babies, that last batch of presents I put in the nursery barely fit. You might lose your room soon, Auntie Remy," Nieko said as they were on their way back from San Diego early Sunday afternoon.

They had a wonderful weekend with Letecia and Brent. Letecia's baby shower was a lot of fun and Brent was still among the living even after telling Letecia he and Nieko were staying for the shower and the food. He had to agree to leave the cookies and homemade egg rolls alone at least until she got hers.

Remisha only had a few moments of sadness thinking of Sarai, the second it hit her, it was as if he knew and Nieko was right by her side, holding her close and whispering how much he loved her and other not so sweet things in her ear. After the baby shower the four of them went to the Brazilian steakhouse for dinner and laughed and talked all night.

"Oh no, I'm not! Me and Letecia have a deal, I get to buy my babies anything I want and it's up to them to figure out where it goes, but I still get to keep my room," Remisha argued, looking rebellious.

Nieko looked at her with an arched eyebrow. Remisha remembered her punishment on the way up and quickly changed her tone, her body was still a little sore from her punishment not to mention her sexual frustration was at an all-time high. Nieko was his sweet and attentive self as usual but he also teased her mercilessly all weekend.

"What time are you going into the office tomorrow?" Nieko asked suddenly, reaching out and moving one of her curls from her face.

Remisha looked at him through her tinted sunglasses so he had soft pink undertones. "I figured I would need a few days to rest and reset after the shower, so it made more sense to work from home for the week."

His sexy smile spread across his face giving her wild thoughts instantly. "Good, because I have a surprise for you and I was going to suggest that anyway. Great minds huh, Remisha?" He grabbed her hand and linked his fingers with hers.

Remisha's face flushed as she smiled bright. "What's the surprise?" she asked excitedly.

Nieko brought her hand to his lips and kissed it softly.

"You'll see," was all he said before turning his focus back to driving.

After several attempts to get him to tell her what the surprise was, she stared out of the window silently pouting until the fatigue she felt from the busy weekend pulled her into an impromptu nap.

"Wake up, beautiful," Nieko whispered in her ear a few hours later, kissing her on the cheek. He wanted to do something very special for her after the shower. Several times over the weekend he noticed her smile didn't quite meet her eyes or he would catch a glimpse of her standing by herself for a few seconds.

He knew her well enough to realize she was hurting, even though she was trying her damnedest to hide it. He knew he couldn't bring Serai back to her but he could love her through the pain she was feeling at the moment.

Nieko watched her as her eyes opened sleepily, slowly she looked around and frowned over at him looking confused.

"Baby, where are we?" she asked, sitting up and looking out at the beach in front of her.

"The Sunset Inn. I wanted to help you unwind a bit. With your job, starting the book, cooking for, planning and hosting the shower, being there for Brent and Letecia and even making time for me, you're taking on the world right now and you need a break," Nieko said leaning across the console, kissing her softly.

He jogged around to her side and helped her out of the car, caught her hand and passed his keys to the valet as they walked into the lobby.

When they walked into their suite, he turned around to see her standing in the middle of the living room with tears in her eyes.

Nieko gathered her into his arms, kissing her again. "Hey, what's that all about?" he asked, looking down at her, smiling.

Remisha wiped her eyes and looked up at him. "You. It's all about you, Nieko. I'm amazed I am blessed enough to have someone like you in my life after so much heartache and pain. Sometimes it's overwhelming that someone as wonderful as you are, wants to be with me," she admitted, dropping her head shyly.

Nieko grasped her chin gently and made her look at him again. "Believe it or not, I feel the same way about you. I know I come off like nothing affects me but I've known hurt and heartache too, not to the extent that you have by any means, but I've had my share of pain. The fact that when your beautiful lips say, 'I love you' it's actually me you're talking to knocks me off center every time. I love you, Remisha and you have become my everything."

Remisha looked out at the water as she and Nieko walked hand in hand on the beach, it was a small walk from their suite.

They decided to take a walk after Nieko found and streamed *"Memoirs of a Geisha"* and they finally finished watching it.

"I will never understand your love of these tragic ass love stories, beautiful. I mean, after everything she went through she finally got to be with the Chairman but not *with* him, so what the hell was the point? That movie was sad as hell," Nieko said, shaking his head looking over at her.

"The book was a lot better and went into a little more detail of what happened next and I guess it's 'the love conquers all' message that I love about the movie and others like that one. I mean no, theirs was not a traditional love, but it was still love they felt for each other and that's all that matters,"

Remisha explained, hating the fact they had to leave in the morning.

The past three days had been some of the best days of her life.

Nieko had arranged massages and champagne on the beach at sunset, breakfast in bed and brought her to so many orgasms she lost count of how many she'd had.

He danced with her on their patio at midnight and even read the first few chapters of her book and gave her honest feedback. She had no idea how it was possible, but she had fallen in love with Nieko all over again and even deeper than before.

He smiled at her as they walked, looking like he was thinking about what she just said. "Reason number 5064 why I love your sexy ass. You find the good in anything or anyone, even that depressing ass movie," he said squeezing her hand tight, before bringing her close for a kiss. "So, it's our last night here, any special requests?" he whispered, holding her close.

"Just keep loving me like you're doing right now," she whispered back, grabbing the back of his head and bringing his lips back to hers.

That was some foul shit you and your boy pulled. Because of you, I lost my fucking job and now I have to relocate. Remisha read the text message from an unknown number twice, getting more confused both times she read it as she chewed on a piece of honeydew melon the next morning.

Who is this? she typed back, putting her phone down and returning to her breakfast.

Nieko set his fork down on the side of his plate. "You good, beautiful?" he asked her with a look of concern settling on his face.

Remisha smiled across the table at him. "Yes, I am blissfully wonderful because of you," she answered, picking up her phone when it vibrated again.

Like you don't know, it's Clinton. I guess killing my daughter wasn't enough huh Remisha?

Remisha smiled as Nieko walked over to her and kissed her briefly before going to take his shower.

When he left the room, her fingers swiped across her keyboard with lightning speed.

First of all, I have no idea what the fuck you are talking about. If you got fired I'm sure that's all on you! Besides, Nieko and I have better things to do than focus on your has been ass! That being said, I don't know how the fuck you got my cellphone number but I'm changing it! Lastly, we both know what happened to Sarai but keep telling yourself whatever you have to to sleep at night. Evaporate! Remisha hit send and went to join Nieko in the shower.

There was no way in hell she was going to let Clinton ruin their last morning in their 'bubble'. She'd tell Nieko about the text messages later.

———

Clinton paced back and forth, his nostrils flaring angrily as he sent Remisha another text. He cut everyone who was talking that dumb shit, telling him to move on already, that Remisha didn't love him and their relationship was all made up in his mind, out of his life.

Melissa was the first one he cut loose, after all these years and the death of his daughter he finally made a choice and he chose Remisha.

Even his fucking boss, someone he once considered a friend, reported him for using his expense account to keep coming to California to see Remisha and got him fired! Disloyal son of a bitch!

Clinton had given up and lost everything to be with her, even after all she did to him, and she had the nerve to act like he didn't fucking exist? Nah, fuck that!

It was like a knife in his heart when he received the restraining order she filed against him, didn't she understand all he was trying to do was love her stupid ass? And she was going to let him damn it, he was tired of this shit!

When he saw she read but didn't answer his previous text, he sent another one and waited, still pacing angrily. She would be home soon enough and then she'd have no choice but to listen!

"Oh my gospel, Remy, please tell me you had a wonderful time, you deserve it!" Letecia exclaimed, when Remisha called her after getting back home. Remisha had to use her house phone, which she hated because she couldn't roam around when she talked, but her cell phone battery was running low after arguing with Clinton all the way from Cambria to Los Angeles via text. So her cellphone was on the charger.

"Lettie, I am practically floating on air, this man, this man, I'm so in love with this man! He treated me like a queen for the last three days, even more so than he usually does! I'm talking massages, dinners, breakfast in bed, dancing at midnight and walking on the beach at sunset. Any and everything I could have asked for, he thought of and did it," Remisha told Letecia, breaking out in a bright smile at the memory of her three day 'runaway' with Nieko.

"Girl, I'm glad you did but let me tell you when you didn't call me Sunday night or Monday morning, I woke Brent up out of a dead sleep and told him he needed to start calling the hospitals and I was going to file a police report because you were missing," Letecia said, giggling at the memory.

"Oh Lettie, please tell you didn't! My poor Broski is getting no peace these days!" Remisha said, laughing at the thought of a very pregnant, very worried Letecia rushing around frantic and waking Brent up because she had not received a phone call.

She went to the kitchen and opened the fridge to figure out something quick to cook for her and Nieko for dinner,

"Your poor, Broski! Girl, I was freaking the hell out, you always call or text me to tell me you made it home," Letecia fussed before giggling again. "Brent kept saying 'She's with Nieko so she's fine, believe me, babe, she's fine'. I guess he knew about Nieko's surprise to steal you away but didn't tell me because he was afraid I would ruin the surprise by getting all excited and spilling the beans. His secretive ass finally told me when he saw me put on my slipper sandals and grab my car keys so I could go find you my damn self!"

The image Letecia just gave her had Remisha laughing very loud and unladylike while she rummaged through the fridge. "Lettie, I swear to God, you are a damn fool! How were you even going to fit behind the damn wheel? You would have had to push the seat all the way to the back seat with all that belly!" she said, shaking her head still chuckling at her silly sister/friend.

Remisha grabbed some smoked turkey and sharp cheddar cheese slices as well as a soft cheese she bought for the shower, but somehow overlooked when she packed up everything to leave on Friday, and some dill out of the crisper, she would make pinwheels for a light dinner.

When she closed the refrigerator door Nieko was standing there glaring at her, his jaw working angrily.

"Uh, Lettie, I'm about to start dinner and I think Nieko needs to talk to me about something, I'm going to call you back in a bit," Remisha said abruptly, trying to figure what the hell could possibly be wrong with Nieko for him to be looking at her that way.

"Okay, Sis. Call me later and tell Nieko I said, 'Hi, Brother-in-law'!" Letecia shouted, hanging up.

Remisha set the pinwheel ingredients on the counter and put the cordless phone back on the charging base and turned back to face Nieko, who still looked pissed and still hadn't said a word. "Letecia told me to tell you 'Hi' and…"

Her train of thought fell away when he placed the 'family' frame from Clinton on the kitchen counter followed by her buzzing cell phone, she picked it up and saw that she had thirty new text messages and seventeen missed calls since she put her phone on the charger. Yeah, Clinton was tripping big time!

"I asked you three times if everything was okay on the way home and not once did you think to tell me this crazy mutha-fucka was blowing up your damn phone like this, why? And then I reach down to pick up the remote and I find this shit? What the fuck is going on, Remisha?" he demanded, his eyes were so dark with anger she couldn't even see the pupils of them.

This wasn't 'you've been disrespectful and you're about to be disciplined' angry Nieko, this was never seen before, 'completely pissed the fuck off, about to lose his shit' Nieko and she had to be completely honest she didn't like him this way at all!

"I-I have no idea how he got my number, but I didn't want him to ruin our last day together before you went back to the office tomorrow. So I was just going to call and get my number changed in the morning and explain to you why I did it, then. I really didn't think it was that serious and he would have gotten bored that I wasn't answering him anymore and stop, to be honest," she explained to him, sitting down on one of her high stools.

Nieko sat down next to her, and pushed the frame closer. "Interesting, not that serious? Baby, first of all, you should have told me he texted as soon as you got the first message and you should have never answered texts from an unknown number at all and blocked his ass! Obviously, it is that serious if he has been sending you semi-threatening messages back-to-back for over four hours now. I told you not to engage this idiot at all because to people like him any attention is good attention. If I didn't know you as well as I do I would have to ask you if you liked the attention or something!" Nieko mused, giving her a disappointed and annoyed look.

Remisha looked at him tilting her head, feeling herself beginning to get angry. "Well, it's a good thing you know me so well then, huh, Nieko? Needless to say, but no, I don't like, or want attention like this from any man. The only man's attention I do want is yours. I thought I was doing the right thing by handling it myself because dealing with Clinton is something you never should have been involved with in the first damn place," she snapped feeling rebellious, she was tired of Clinton and his fucking power play bullshit and she hated that in spite of how she tried to avoid it, he was ruining her time with Nieko with his craziness any damn way!

Nieko still looked ready to kill but his eyebrow arched at her tone as he moved the frame closer to her. "Well, I am involved but that's not the point, at the moment. Where did this come from?" he asked her, his face was serious and stoic. She really didn't like this side of Nieko and wanted this conversation to be over!

Remisha picked it up and put it face down on the bar. "The day he sent the small picture to you, he sent this one to me. I was on the phone with Lettie and she was getting upset when I mentioned Clinton had sent me something else, she got so pissed, I regretted even calling her about it. I was afraid she would make herself and the babies sick so I quickly downplayed it, said I could handle it and never told her what he sent me. I set the stupid thing on the side of the couch while we finished talking, then you got here and you were pissed off, carrying around a picture of your own and I completely forgot about it," Remisha told him quietly, still feeling frustrated that after four months and especially after such a wonderful three days they had circled back to Clinton and his fucking drama.

Nieko sat there and watched her quietly for what seemed like an eternity before he let out a sigh of relief. "Remisha, I thought he left this in your house, my next move was to find his ass," he admitted, his smile returning.

Remisha blinked and smiled nervously. "You weren't mad at me? That violent and murderous glare is for Clinton, not me?" she asked, feeling relieved that the amount of animosity that was coming off Nieko wasn't directed at her.

"Beautiful, I don't ever think I could ever be that angry with you, but I am upset you didn't tell me he was texting you. You are so quick to say, things aren't that serious but to me if I'm bringing them up, then they are that serious. To be honest, I think you know they are serious, too but you are just so used to downplaying your emotions, wants, and needs that phrase is your go to so you won't appear disappointed," he said, taking her hands in his. "Remisha, when are you going to understand that since meeting you, your happiness and wellbeing are the most important things to me? Even though he didn't bring it into your house, the fact he sent it in that frame with the intent of breaking you down even further than he did before, makes me want to break his fucking neck," he said with a growl, his jaw jumped angrily again.

"Well, aren't you the lucky one, because here I am, Nemo!" Clinton shouted, stepping into the kitchen from her patio, his eyes were wide and crazy, his nostrils flared.

Clinton saw the look of surprise on their faces and smiled triumphantly. "I was hoping you and I could have a one-on-one conversation, Remy but since we're all here, why don't you stop playing with Nemo's emotions once and for all and tell him what's up," he said moving further into the kitchen. He noticed Nemo, or whatever the hell his name was, had stood up and was standing in front of Remisha, his big ass was completely blocking her from his view.

"What's up is you are fucking crazy, Clinton! How the hell did you even get in my backyard, let alone my house?" he heard Remisha ask. He needed to see her face, she sounded upset but he couldn't understand why, he was here just like she wanted.

Clinton moved to come up behind her and 'Nemo' stepped in his way again, this cock-blocking giant of a man was getting on his fucking nerves!

"Ay, you know what, man, if you and me need to throw hands to get you out of the way let's do this shit!" Clinton rushed forward in a fight stance, he hoped Remisha could finally see how much she meant to him, he was willing to fight for her and he had all the tools he needed to win too!

Nieko's mind was going a mile a minute, he didn't like being caught off guard, all he was thinking was he needed to figure out a way to get Remisha out of the kitchen and away from the knife he saw clutched in Clinton's hand.

It was safe to say the seemingly well put together looking man Nieko had seen over four months ago was gone, in that time it appeared Clinton had lost his mind! Clinton rushed up, his hand not holding the knife was balled up and he dropped back in a fighting stance.

"Leave," Nieko said to Remisha over his shoulder, keeping

his eyes on Clinton the entire time. Remisha slipped off of the tall chair quickly and moved out of his line of sight, he prayed she would leave the house and call 911.

"Remisha! Get your ass back here!" Clinton yelled and took a wild swing at Nieko with the knife.

Nieko successfully dodged the blade intended for his face and got into his own stance, he swung at Clinton and clipped him on the chin. He watched Clinton stumble back but regain his balance and swing at him again with the knife missing him by inches.

"I don't even understand why the fuck you're even here, 'Nemo'! You have a snowball's chance in Hell of replacing me! I'm Remisha's first love, her only love!" Clinton yelled, swinging again, his eyes were wide and wild. "I know you're the one who made her get a restraining order too, couldn't stand the competition, huh?" Clinton spat, his eyes were red and almost seemed like they had a mind of their own as they darted around in his sockets.

Nieko scoffed at Clinton and dodged him again. "You're really outside of your right mind, man. That woman doesn't want anything to do with you, period. She was done with your ass before I even came on the scene." He didn't want to agitate Clinton any more than he already was but maybe keeping him talking would distract him enough to get the knife.

"Bullshit! Remisha! Get in here! Get in here and tell this man who your heart belongs to! Tell him how you told me you would love me and only me, forever! You remember that, baby?" Clinton screamed over his shoulder in the direction Remisha had fled.

Nieko stepped in while Clinton's head was slightly turned and connected with his mouth knocking him down on his ass, taking the knife from him. "Bruh, you have got to let that shit go, man. I don't know what's going on in your head but what y'all had been is over, man, like for years. I get it, it's hard to see the one that got away moving on but you gotta face facts, it's over," Nieko explained to Clinton, while standing over him, watching his crazy ass closely just in case he tried to get up again.

Clinton glared up at Nieko, blood dripping from his from his busted face. "Man, fuck that, this ain't over! She just needed time to get over shit! That's why she wrote that story, it was letting me know she was ready for us to try again!" Clinton argued spitting blood on Remisha's floor, he tried to get up and slid back down on his ass.

"So, let me get this right, you were giving her time to 'get over shit' as you so eloquently put it in regard to her losing her child and her ability to procreate in the same damn day? Then you think, after all she's been through, she sent you a signal through a short story to tell you she wanted to get back together, instead of just calling you or something simple like that? And the minute you find out that's not the case and she doesn't react the way you expected her to, you throw her losing a child all up in her face, especially the part where you accused her of killing the baby you know, good and damn well, you didn't want in the first place? You and I both know Sarai would have been just another weapon you used to try to control Remisha but that's beside the point. You claim to have done this all in the name of love? Is that really what love is to you?" Nieko asked calmly, looking down at Clinton like the piece of shit he was as far as he was concerned.

"She did kill my daughter! Remisha took her away from me because I was still messing with Melissa and she couldn't take not being the only one in my life! I don't give a fuck what she told you! Remisha killed her, it's all her fault! She lost our baby acting fucking stupid with Letecia's stuck up ass!" Clinton screamed trying to stand again before he fell back down. "She told me Melissa attacked her because of me, because of the lies I told, but that's not true, that's not fucking true!" he cried out like a wounded animal and started babbling and wailing.

"Remisha! This is all your fault! If you hadn't tried to leave me Sarai would be here, don't you understand that? You killed our daughter!"

Nieko watched him getting pale and struggling to stand and fail again with alarm, he knew he hit him hard but not so hard that he couldn't stand again. And for the first time Nieko had to wonder what in the hell was this fool on?

A split second later his stomach dropped in fear as he saw Remisha rounding the corner and angrily rushing back into the kitchen.

"For the last fucking time, Clinton, Melissa pushed me down the stairs and kicked me in the stomach! She hated me because of you and all the lies you told her! You and your fucking ego killed Sarai! You Clinton, not me! I know I told you I forgave you but I will go to my fucking grave hating your ass for it! *I hate you Clinton Maxwell! I fucking hate you! You killed her! You killed my baby!*" Remisha sobbed as she came further into the kitchen, she grabbed the 'family' picture frame and threw it at Clinton's head before dropping to her knees, hugging herself and crying. "Don't you dare say her name! She was mine, not yours, she was mine and you took her from me because you couldn't have me!" She sobbed as she rocked back and forth on her knees. "I can never have babies and it's all your fucking fault! Just disappear and leave me the fuck alone!" she yelled at Clinton, kicking a piece of the broken picture frame in his direction.

Nieko rushed forward to comfort Remisha and looked up in time to see Clinton's eyes roll back inside his head as he slumped over, knocked out cold by the picture frame. Damn, his baby had good aim and follow through, something he would make sure to remember in the future in case he ever pissed her off.

Remisha felt Nieko gather her in his arms as she cried and carry her into the living room and away from Clinton. "Beautiful, one day you are going to actually listen the first time I tell you to do something, I swear you are, but we will discuss that later. Right now, please tell me you at least called 911 so we can get this blathering idiot the hell off your kitchen floor," he said, using his thumbs to wipe her tears away.

Remisha nodded still crying. "I did listen! I left the house just like you told me to. I went to the back yard and called 911 but when I saw how he cut up my patio furniture and found the gun and lines of cocaine on the table back there, I came back inside," she told him through her sobs. "I couldn't leave you in here with him knowing he was high off his ass and crazy as hell! I heard him screaming at you and all I kept thinking was he wasn't going to take you away from me too, I didn't want to lose you, too!" She broke down and fell against Nieko crying again.

"Baby, I understand, but I was a lot safer in here alone than I was with you in this house because then I had two people I was trying to keep safe. You are just as important to me as I am to you, when are you going to actually realize that?" Nieko asked her, holding her close.

Remisha shrugged and moved closer to him and gave a prayer of thanks when she heard sirens approaching.

Clinton slowly opened his eyes and looked around trying to remember what happened. The rhythmic beep of a heart monitor welcomed him back to consciousness, he tried to move his hand and found that he was handcuffed to the bed and panicked, what the fuck was going on?

"Nurse! Help, I need a nurse!" he shouted at the top of his lungs, the last thing he remembered was waiting for Remisha to come home so how the hell did he end up in the hospital handcuffed to a bed?

A gray-haired nurse, built like a linebacker, stepped into the room, followed by Remisha's boyfriend, Nemo or whatever the hell his name was.

"Damn man, I was beginning to think you were never going to wake up," Nieko said sitting down on the chair next to the bed.

Clinton looked over at the nurse. "What the fuck is this dude doing in my room, man? You just waltzed in here like HIPAA ain't a thing and shit?" he demanded rolling his eyes at Nieko.

The linebacker nurse ignored him and continued checking the monitors and making notes. Nieko patiently waited scrolling on his phone while she worked looking completely unbothered by Clinton's outburst.

"Ain't this about a bitch? How the fuck her dresser shaped ass gonna just ignore me like that?" Clinton snapped as he watched the nurse finish her notes, smile at Nieko and leave the room, closing the door behind her.

"Well, that's what happens when you're on the jail side of the hospital, bedside manner goes out the window, I guess." Nieko sighed and tucked his phone in his inside jacket pocket.

"By the way, the reason why they let me back here is because I told them you were my brother and our mother was sick. You know they think we all look alike any damn way so I figured it was as good of an excuse as any," Nieko informed him, looking at him with a shit eating grin.

Clinton thought he couldn't stand Nemo's ass before but yeah he hated this cocky motherfucker! "Look, Nemo, or whatever the fuck your name is, I am in no fucking mood for you or your bullshit, I just woke up handcuffed to a bed with a fucking headache and I have no idea why, so you got about five seconds to get the fuck out of my hospital room before I snap!" Clinton threatened, glaring at Nieko.

"Now see that's where I come in, I can answer all of that for you. You are handcuffed to the bed because you are now in the custody of the State of California Department of Corrections for violating a protection order, possession of an illegal firearm, breaking and entering, attempted assault with a deadly weapon and possession of a controlled substance. Whew! I think that's it. Thank God, Remisha doesn't have a pet, they probably would have charged you with animal cruelty too, just because," Nieko said, taking an exaggerated deep breath. "Now your headache is a three-part story, it comes from your overdose and almost death from aforementioned controlled substance, the jab I threw that busted your lip and broke your tooth, and lastly from the heavy ass glass picture frame Remisha launched at your head in a fit of rage so, yeah I can only imagine your head is probably thumping right about now."

Clinton jerked at his handcuffs trying to get to Nieko. "Man, keep playing with me if you want to! Get the fuck out of my room!" he yelled, jerking his body on the bed tantrum style.

"Oh, trust me, you will get your wish soon enough but first, you and I are going to have a little talk, or better yet I'm going to talk and you're going to listen," Nieko informed Clinton, sounding far more calm than he looked.

"Man, whatever, Nemo, I ain't trying to hear a mutha-fucking thing you got to say," Clinton said, rolling his eyes at Nieko.

"That's another thing, my name is Nieko, Nee-Ko, you might want to remember it since I'm the man who will be marrying your Baby Momma," Nieko paused and waited for what he just said to sink in. Clinton glared over at him like he wanted to kill him.

"Yeah, you heard me. I've waited all my life for a woman like Remisha and now that I've found her, I have no intention of letting her go. I've waited three days for you to come out of that coma to tell you our happy news and that you will be letting her go right here, right now. This bullshit obsession and harassment ends today, she will not shed another tear because of you and the shit you did to her, you hear me? If you write a letter, send a text, make a phone call or even blink in her direction again, you will have me to deal with and trust me, not even prison bars will keep me off your goofy ass, you feel me?" Nieko asked standing up to leave.

"Fuck you, *Nee-mo*! I don't give a fuck who she loves, who she marries, we will always be connected in a way no other man can ever connect with her, so good luck with that, playa!" Clinton spat, looking Nieko up and down like the joke he thought he was. Gonna try to come into his hospital room, tossing around charges and threats like he was Charlie Badass!

Nieko chuckled and strolled towards the door before looking back at Clinton. "Now see that's the difference between a man like me and a man-child like you. You stay stuck in the past, playing a constant loop of 'remember when', you try to coast by on the few good things you did for a woman forever, hoping she never needs or asks for more than your half-assed efforts and attempts of love. A man like me on the other hand is in a constant state of motion, the minute I do something to make my woman smile, I'm already thinking of what I can do next to top it. Because I love to see her happy and causing her any kind of pain is the furthest thing from my mind." Nieko knocked to be let out of the room. "You're right, Remisha and I will never know the joy of sharing biological children but let's be quite honest Clinton you never knew that joy either, your girl Melissa made sure of that. However, I will get to see Remisha as a mother and be by her side as we raise our kids together while you will still be holding on to a sick badge of honor regarding a child you all but tore from her mother's arms before she even had a chance to live. Sarai's memory will always live on just not as the sick mockery you've made of it. Rest easy, brother, I know we will." Nieko winked at Clinton and stepped out the door.

"Guess he didn't take the news about Mom so well." Nieko shrugged as he walked past the nurses' station and their confused faces as Clinton yelled and screamed profanities while the heavy metal door to his room slowly closed.

He had just stepped off the elevator and was making his way out the front doors of the hospital when his phone rang, "Hey, beautiful, I was just about to call you," he said to her as soon as answered his phone, putting on his sunglasses. He pulled the ring box he picked up before his visit to Clinton out of his pocket and smiled down at the yellow diamond. He couldn't wait for her to be his wife, to wake up next to her every day surrounded by her love would be his dream come true.

"Baby, it's Lettie! I got to get to San Diego, it looks like she's having the babies! The babies are coming!" Remisha told him, sounding excited and out of breath.

"I'm on my way, and try to relax, I will do everything in my power to get you there in time and don't even fix your sexy ass lips to argue with me about it."

"Fine, Nieko, see you soon." Remisha rolled her eyes and closed her mouth. As she hung up the phone, her words of protest were still dancing on her tongue dying for a chance to be heard.

In true form, Nieko took charge, she knew him driving her to San Diego was not up for negotiation. Honestly, she didn't have a problem with it, she knew that's what would happen when she called him anyway. She had finally gotten used to Nieko's protective, yet demanding ways and she wouldn't want him to be any other way.

Nieko had become her confidant, her lover, her everything in the short time since they met and her heart soared as she thought of the love they shared. He was her peace and the reason for her calm and she thanked God every day for bringing a man like him into her life.

Epilogue

Two and a half years later

Remisha sat on her bed smiling at the TV as Major Gruver swept Hana-Ogi away from the reporters and off to get married. As much as she still loved getting lost in her tragic love stories she loved her reality even more.

What was once a life full of regrets and bitter reminders of the past was now a life filled with laughter and love. Her good times strongly outweighed the bad, as a matter-of-fact bad times were practically non-existent in her life now because she never allowed them to hang around for long.

In the past two and a half years, Remisha had taken an honest and hard look at her life and made the changes necessary to be and stay happy.

She never did feel comfortable again in 'the dollhouse' after that crazy afternoon with Clinton, so shortly after the triplets were born, she put her once beloved house on the market and much to Brent and Letecia's delight, she ended up buying a new house in San Diego about forty-five minutes from where they lived.

They were all impressed that Nieko made it for an entire six months in Los Angeles without her before he announced that he was relocating, too. Not that it came as a surprise since he spent all his time with Remisha in San Diego anyway and they had a brand-new city to get lost in, so it made perfect sense.

Two days after her nieces and nephew hit the fifteen-months-old mark, she became Mrs. Nieko King. Four months later, she finished her first novel which was met with lots of success, not New York Times Bestseller kind of success but she was still proud of how well it did. She now had plans to write a sequel at some point but in the meantime, Remisha kept her job as an editor working remotely full time and still wrote short stories from time to time. She traveled to Los Angeles for staff meetings and other important engagements but it just really didn't seem like home to her anymore.

Nieko opened three more African Gift stores in San Diego and they were all doing quite well. He still owned and ran his company and kept his house in Los Angeles in case he or Remisha needed to stay overnight for their jobs and he also rented it out as an Airbnb from time to time as well.

Remisha was finally able to talk openly about Sarai and she even hung the shadow box, Letecia made for her right after Sarai passed, in her office.

There were still times when she would shed tears and mourn her daughter's passing but Nieko, Letecia, Brent and the triplets were there to help her through it.

Last she heard, Clinton was serving out his twenty-five-year prison sentence in Crowley, Colorado. Apparently he had been wanted for other charges besides the ones in California including grand larceny and fraud. He never even crossed her mind much anymore, she was too busy loving life and being adored by her handsome husband.

From the beginning of their relationship she always counted herself lucky because of the way Nieko treated her, now as his wife she knew how truly blessed she really was. To be loved and adored by a man who was truly committed to making his wife happy was nothing short of amazing and she basked in his love every day.

"TeeTee!" Remisha's identical twin nieces Reign and Ryleigh rushed into Remisha and Nieko's room, the credits rolling on her movie.

The triplets surprised them all when they were born, the entire time Letecia was pregnant, everyone thought three separate babies in three separate sacs but when they were delivered by C-section it was discovered that the girls were actually identical and shared one sac and Rory was in the other one.

Nieko always teased her and said he didn't know who was more excited about their monthly visits to their house, the babies or Remisha with the way she always made sure to have fun things planned for them all to do.

"TeeTee's Princesses are here!" Remisha squealed in an excited voice opening her arms, the girls both threw their arms around Remisha's neck as she hugged them close both babbling with a few English words thrown in at the same time.

"Girl, I promise you they just know when we are coming over here. I swear I can barely keep them in their car seats when we turn on to your street anymore!" Letecia said, walking into her room carrying three tiny suitcases. She sat on the bed next to Remisha, looking like she never had one baby, let alone three, she looked casually sharp as always.

The first thing the girls did when Letecia brought them over when they learned how to walk was go down the hall to find their 'TeeTee'. Rory usually went right to the kitchen and pointed at the cookie jar before running off to watch sports with his Uncle Nieko clutching his treat in his hand.

"Yeah, well my little princesses know TeeTee Remy and Uncle Nieko's house is much more fun than Mommy and Daddy's house! Huh pretty girls?" Remisha asked the twins hugging them close again and shrugged her shoulders at Letecia's deadpan look. Reaching out, she helped the girls climb up on the bed. "Rory in the kitchen?" she asked needlessly, helping Reign out of her jacket.

"Girl you already know he is, him and his damn daddy are cookie fiends, I swear!" Letecia answered, taking Ryleigh's jacket off too and handing it to Remisha. "I keep telling Brent we gotta keep that boy in sports or he will be huge!"

Remisha pushed Letecia on the shoulder. "Girl, don't be putting that on my baby! It's not his fault that all your evil ass craved was butter cookies and was willing to go to war to get them! He's fine, besides with Brent and Nieko around he will probably be in the gym by the time he's three. You know how they are with all their alpha male bull crap and antics," Remisha said, referring to the time that Brent and Nieko tried to outlift each other the first time they went to the gym together and both came home limping and sore as hell.

"True, it's just crazy to think about sometimes, Rory is so much like Brent and the girls are like my carbon copies," Letecia said, passing Remisha the girls' shoes; if an adult did not take them off and put them away, good luck finding them when they needed them to go somewhere.

"It's not weird, Lettie it's called genetics, crazy!" Remisha quipped turning her head towards a small sound on the other side of the bedroom

Once the girls were comfortable, they climbed off the bed and walked hand in hand and peeked over the edge of the bassinet where Remisha and Nieko's four-month-old, adopted daughter Calista was waking up from her nap.

When they first adopted her, everyone was afraid the triplets might not adjust well to not being the only babies anymore, but the girls fell in love with her instantly. Rory, in typical boy fashion, was pretty much indifferent.

Remisha and Nieko met Calista's birth mother nine months after they were married. The ink on their adoption application barely had time to dry before they were being contacted to meet her.

Syryn was a twenty-two-year-old college student who wanted to finish school, and felt she was too young to be a mother and wanted to do what she felt was best for her baby.

Remisha loved her sweet and calm demeanor immediately and couldn't believe it when Syryn selected them to adopt her baby. Syryn insisted on a closed adoption. She placed Calista in Remisha's arms herself and signed over her rights with no hesitation the moment Calista was born.

The last thing Syryn did for her daughter before she told her goodbye forever was name her as the three of them agreed upon very early on in the process. She told them she chose the name 'Calista' because it meant 'beautiful' in Greek and since that was what she always heard Nieko call Remisha, she thought it was fitting.

"Speaking of princesses, how is mine?" Letecia asked softly, tiptoeing over to the bassinet to pick Calista up. Everything Letecia ever bought for Sarai was brought over and added to Calista's nursery right after she was born.

Remisha and Letecia shed a lot of tears that day, they were tears of joy mixed with tears of sadness. Sadness because of the tragic way Sarai was taken from them and tears of joy because another beautiful baby girl had joined the family.

"She is so beautiful, Remy. I know you get tired of hearing it from me and you're going to say it's not possible again but I still say she looks a lot like you and Nieko," Letecia said, squatting down so the girls could see the baby.

"Lettie, I can't even argue with you about it anymore because you're not the only who says that, everywhere we go someone is commenting on how much she looks like a perfect blend of us, I guess that goes to show God really is the best of all planners," Remisha replied, hanging up the girls' jackets in the closet before coming and peeking over Letecia's shoulder at her daughter.

Nieko leaned on the doorframe and watched Remisha as she rocked Calista back to sleep later the same night.

He was proud of himself because he had successfully got all three of the triplets into pajamas and in bed by himself and didn't feel like he got his ass handed to him in the process. He was also happy he didn't miss watching his two beautiful ladies in their night time ritual.

"Beautiful, why do you sing that depressing ass song to our daughter every single night?" Nieko asked her, shaking his head with a smile. He wandered inside Calista's nursery and closer to them. Every night Remisha sang the song *"Sayonara"* to their daughter until she fell asleep.

She looked over at him giving him a deadpan look, with her eyes narrowed. "I'm programing her early so you are destined to be surrounded by beautiful women who force you to watch tragic love stories," she snapped with a smirk. Remisha watched *"Sayonara"* and *"Memoirs of a Geisha"* so much that even her nieces loved watching them too.

He raised an eyebrow and squatted in front of the rocking chair she and Calista were sitting on, "Oh really?" he asked in that subtle way that told her she was pushing it. "Do we need to discuss your attitude, Mrs. King?" he asked her, leaning forward and kissing both her and Calista on the forehead softly.

Remisha felt her middle react immediately and jump in response to what he was alluding to, she was always up for one of Nieko's games of discipline.

"Easy Mr. Gamemaster, I need to make sure your daughter is completely asleep before you even think of going there and we have three other babies here, too, so you're going to have to show me a little mercy," she said, leaning forward and pressing her lips to his before standing up to put the baby in her crib. "And to answer your question seriously, I sing *"Sayonara"* to our daughter every night so she always believes in love and, like the women in those movies, she will know that despite all the tragedies she might have to go through to get there, true love always finds a way," she explained with her eyes filling with happy tears. "After all, my tragedies helped me find you."

Nieko walked up next to the crib and waited until she had the baby all tucked in before taking her by the hand and leading her out of Calista's room, grabbing the baby monitor on their way out.

"That's all well and good, thanks for finally answering my question, but too little, too late. So now we're going to have a little talk about your smart-ass mouth, and all of that BS about mercy? Miss me with that, like I always say, you know what you did so own that shit! Now what's the safe word?" he whispered to her, closing the door to their room, and pulling her night-gown off over her head, his dark eyes flashing intensely before he backed away from her in the direction of his 'toy closet'.

Remisha stood exactly where he left her completely naked, watching him grab a few things from his closet before coming back to her, looking at her expectantly. She knew her husband well enough to know he was waiting for her to answer him now that he was ready to begin.

She took a deep breath as he fastened a silk covered hand-cuff to one of her wrists, then the other and fought to keep the excitement she felt from showing on her face when she looked up at him and answered, "Chocolate."

The End

Joy Bussu

Blessings! I am 48-year-old Joy Bussu. Eighteen years married, mother of four, grandmother of one. I was born in Wichita Falls, Texas, but raised in Denver, Colorado, where I currently reside with my beautiful family.

I have always had a love for the written word. I devoured books from the time I could string sentences together and I have always loved to write. Once I gave birth to my youngest child and only daughter, I was finally ready to attempt to write my first book. It took me over ten years to complete it.

Holding the first copy of my self-published book was the opening of the flood gate I never even realized I was holding back. Writing is my passion and my life and it is my pleasure and deepest honor to be able to share it with the world. My dream is to touch as many as humanly possible with my work.

Visit my webpage

Don't miss these exciting titles by Joy Bussu and Blushing Books!

Nieko's Treasure
Whispers
Makia's Bodyguard

Anthologies
12 Naughty Days of Christmas 2020

Blushing Books

Blushing Books is one of the oldest eBook publishers on the web. We've been running websites that publish spanking and BDSM related romance and erotica since 1999, and we have been selling eBooks since 2003. We hope you'll check out our hundreds of offerings at http://www.blushingbooks.com.

Blushing Books Newsletter

Please join the Blushing Books newsletter
to receive updates & special promotional offers.
You can also join by using your mobile phone:
Just text BLUSHING to 22828.